Cowboy Up

Welcome to my special boxed set with the first two books from two separate cowboy series! Up first, HER COWBOY HERO, book 1 of my Cowboys of Ransom Creek series and a free chapter of book 2, THE COWBOY'S BRIDE FOR HIRE right after.

Up next is HER TEXAS COWBOY, book 1 of my New Horizon Ranch series with a free chapter of book 2, RAFE.

I hope you enjoy this book with access to both my bestselling cowboy series. Get ready to COWBOY UP and I hope you have a great reading experience.

Debra Clopton

COWBOY UP COLLECTION

Her Cowboy Hero
Her Texas Cowboy

DEBRA CLOPTON

Contents

HER COWBOY HERO

Cowboys of Ransom Creek, Book One

CHAPTER ONE

"The horses in the trailer are gone."

What? Lori Calhoun stared at Trip Jensen, her foreman at the Calhoun Ranch and also her partner in the rough stock rodeo contracting business—thanks to her father.

The pit of her stomach knotted as she saw the solemn look in Trip's eyes.

"All five of them?" she asked, fighting the shock of finding out their prized saddle broncs had been stolen.

Trip shifted his weight from one boot to the other. His handsome features twisted with disgust and fury as he squinted at her from beneath the straw Stetson shading his light blue eyes. "Yep. They're gone. But we will find them. Harvey and Mike said they loaded the horses on the trailer before they connected it to the truck. Don't ask me why they did that. Then they went to get the truck—which was for some reason still on the other side of the arena. When they got back the trailer loaded with our horses had disappeared."

She blinked through frustrations strangling her. "That doesn't even sound right. What was Harvey thinking?"

"I don't know," Trip bit out, showing his frustration. "I have no reason to believe that he or Mike had anything to do with the theft—other than lack of good judgement. But I'm looking into it just the same."

Her stomach churned. Those were her champion rodeo Broncs and the mainstay of the rough stock business. Those horses were heading to the Western Rodeo Circuit Finals if they kept performing like they were this year. They were the cornerstone of the business but she didn't need to tell Trip that. Like her, he had a stake in this business and understood all too well how important it was for their horses to be in the finals this year. So much had happened this year, her father had died in a tragic horse accident which that alone still held her in the grips of grief. But on top of that, everyone would be watching to see if she and Trip could continue with the tradition of Calhoun stock in the WRC finals that had begun from the first year her daddy had formed the stock contracting business. Trip had bought half the company only three months before Ray Calhoun's horse threw him and he hit his head and died and left her to take the reins of the ranch and the other half of the stock company. And Lori was struggling.

Add to that her mounting frustration at being forced, by her dad, to work with Trip.

Those frustrations had been mounting for the last five

months, threatening to explode and now this…she swung around to stare out the window. Fighting anger and insecurities she slammed her fists to her hips and studied the barns and arenas across the wide yard and gravel parking area. This was the ranch her daddy had built. The ranch that now rested on her shoulders and she felt in every way that she was not living up to expectations.

"Daddy would've been furious right now," she said.

He'd been dead only five months. Her heart ached and she felt like she was in over her head. He would be rolling over his grave right now if he knew that on her watch she'd lost such a legacy.

"It's not your fault, Lori. It's not mine either. Someone did this and we're going to find out who. It's that simple. Your dad wouldn't be mad at you. Them— yes. No doubt about that."

She spun back to glare at Trip. "This happened on my watch—and so did that trailer load of steers that someone just drove off the property with last week."

"Lori Lyn Calhoun I'm warning you to stop blaming yourself. You didn't lose those broncs or that load of steers. It's only a matter of time before we catch them. Those rangers will get a lead on them. As for the load of horses, Harvey and Mike lost them on *my* watch. And I plan to find them."

"Our watch," she snapped, stubbornly. "Do you think Harvey and Mike are guilty?"

"Of carelessness. But until I get better answers as to why they loaded that trailer and then left it unattended with our prized stock in it, I'm not going to be easy to live with. And they won't be careless like that again."

She took a deep breath and tried to hold onto her show of strength but the façade was growing thin. Since her dad's death, she felt so alone. Her mother had turned her back on her when she was a baby and it had just been her and her dad. And then, there was Trip…she pushed away the overpowering wish to feel his strong arms around her. Once things had been so easy between them. Once that would have been an option.

But it hadn't been for a very long time. "So, what do we do now?" she asked instead of gaining strength from him.

"I've called the cops and reported it. I've also called the Knight Investigation Agency—since they know the rodeo and investigate incidents for the WRC, they might be able to find out more than the police. They only asked Harvey and Mike a couple of questions then told them they'd be in touch if they hear anything. The Knights have taken the lead since this was a WRC sanctioned rodeo."

"That's good to know. I've met all three brothers, Jesse, Sean and Michael. They're great. And their dad and mine competed against each other in their younger years in the rodeo."

"I think they'll get to the bottom of it."

She bit her lip. "This will be a first that the Calhoun Ranch or the stock company has ever been in the middle of a rodeo investigation."

She didn't think that was a fluke. No, her dad, Ray Calhoun, had been one tough cowboy. He'd built this ranch and the rough stock business from the ground up and he was as tough as the bucking horses they bred. Her daddy was a hard businessman, a hard rider, and a harder man when it came to being crossed.

"There's a first for everything," Trip said. "But that doesn't mean we have to like it or take it."

"Right," she grunted. "I'm pretty certain nobody messed with Daddy simply because of who he was." But she wasn't her daddy. She was just his daughter trying hard to step into his boots and knowing no one could ever replace him. She fought off the sudden need to cry and wished she still had her back to Trip.

"You're doing a good job, Lori," he said and took a step toward her but stopped. "Your dad would be proud of you for sticking around and stepping in for him."

For a brief moment, it felt like it once had, when things were easy between them…before everything had gotten so complicated.

She sighed. "I'm trying. But this isn't helping." She wanted desperately to live up to the expectation of her dad…her daddy. He deserved only the best she could give because that was what he'd always given to her.

When Lori was two her mother ran off with another man and hadn't wanted anything to do with Lori or her dad. He had tried to love her enough for himself and her runaway mother and that had meant he'd spoiled her in many ways but he'd raised her to be independent too. And when eventually she'd chosen to take a job in Houston instead of staying here and running the ranch with him, he'd given her his blessing. She'd been in Houston when she'd gotten the call that he was dead.

Devastated had been too small a word for what she'd felt. What she still felt.

She still carried the wound that she'd not been here on the ranch where she belonged when he'd had his accident. She didn't think she would ever get over that.

And now this.

She focused on Trip, standing solid and strong as he waited for her to speak. For only a moment she wished again that she could rest her head on his shoulder and feel the support of his arms around her…but she pushed that thought out of her mind. This was not the time for regrets or a show of weakness. Instead, she pushed her shoulders back and yanked her big girl pants uptight—she was Ray Calhoun's daughter. "What did the Knights say? Fill me in and let's get on this. I do not plan to stand by and let vultures start pecking off bits and pieces of my daddy's legacy."

Trip smiled. "Well, hello, Lori Calhoun. Where the dickens have you been lately?"

Her heart clenched. "Having a pity party. And I just realized my daddy raised me better than that."

She thought she saw approval in Trip's gaze. "The police said they'll call if they hear anything. They're on the lookout for the trailer, though I'm not holding out any hope since whoever did this probably changed the plates.

If not, then I figure the trailer will be found abandoned somewhere empty. As for the Knights, Sean Knight was at the rodeo in case a veterinarian was needed since that's his job. He'd already left the grounds but is hanging around the area and not flying home since the next WRC rodeo is in Fort Worth at the Stockyards next week. So, he's supposed to meet me at the arena in Mesquite at three."

"Great. I'll join you, then," she said, glancing at her watch. "When are we leaving?"

"It's a two-hour drive from Ransom Springs to the arena so how about right after lunch?"

"Perfect. I'll meet you at the truck at one."

"Sounds good. I better go to my office and get a few things done," he said, then without another word headed out the door of her daddy's office. Her office.

Unable to stop herself she moved to the window and watched him move with purposeful strides across the yard toward the stables that also housed the ranch manager's office—his office.

A decade-old longing seeped over her. Their relationship was complicated. And she'd learned to live with things the way they were years ago after he'd headed off to college and left her behind. She'd thought she might one day get over him, had hoped she would.

And then her daddy had hired him on as manager and gone into business with him.

And then he'd complicated things more by dying and leaving her here to sort things out.

Complicated, her life in a nutshell.

It took everything Trip had in him to walk out of that house without pulling Lori into his arms and try to comfort her. She was being too hard on herself, having lost her dad and then stepping into the ownership of the ranch and the rodeo stock company. She had a lot on her shoulders and trying to live up to the expectations of her father or others expectations was not making things any easier. And then dealing with him as ranch manager…things had been strained between them ever since she'd come home from Houston to deal with the ranch's needs after Ray's death.

She had a life in Houston and he wasn't certain if she planned to go back to that life when things were sorted out here or if she planned to stay.

One thing he knew, his time was running out to bridge this canyon between them. And the horses being stolen wasn't helping anything. It was just adding more burden on her already loaded down shoulders.

He hurt for her. It was hard knowing his being here was adding more strain on her. It was hard on him too. But, he was determined to help her. And to make things right between them.

CHAPTER TWO

Sean Knight showed up at the Mesquite arena on time. Lori and Trip had made the two-hour drive and arrived just before him.

Despite all that they had going on, she found that inside the close quarters of the truck that awkwardness that had been between them since she'd taken over the ranch intensified. The close quarters seemed to draw in on her and she was so aware of him as a man that it was very nearly overwhelming.

She'd managed to keep up a stilted conversation about ranch business and how best to cope with the loss of the missing horses. The man smelled entirely too good but, she managed not to sigh or inhale in desperate gulps. Unrequited love was the pits. Pure and simple it was torture. She'd kept her end of the conversation flowing but no matter how hard she tried, their unfinished business from high school hung in the air between them like an elephant clinging to a tightrope.

They'd been the best of friends growing up…then they'd matured. The fact that she'd wanted more than friendship from him, she'd wanted a life with him. He hadn't wanted the same thing and it had been hard to get over. But she had.

And then her dad had thrown them together again.

When they reached the Mesquite rodeo arena, she almost threw herself out of the truck in her desperation to get away. She'd never been so thankful to be out of the close confines of the truck in all of her life. Trip smelled too good, his voice sounded too good—and none of that kind of thinking was good for her.

No, those kinds of thoughts would do nothing but cause her misery and right now, with her dad's loss she had enough of that to deal with.

Sean Knight was waiting for them. Sean held out his hand to Trip and they shook, then his sympathetic gaze touched her. "We were all sorry to hear about your dad. He was a good man."

"Thank you. It's still so hard to believe but I'm doing okay. I was blessed to have him in my life. But you know how that is. My dad always liked your dad. He would be so proud of all of you."

"Thanks. Now let's take a look around. These horses disappearing like this from the rodeo is pretty bold."

"Tell me about it," Trip agreed. "Who would just hook up to someone else's trailer and drive off. I guess it being dark helped."

"Probably so. And it was busy so maybe no one

would have paid attention but then again, maybe someone did. We'll see what we can dig up by asking around. Can you tell me what you know?"

Trip filled him in about Harvey and Mike and everything they knew so far. She followed them to the spot where the trailer had last been sitting. The area was dirt with various tracks all around including the markings of where their trailer had been parked. But all around there were very near identical markings from where all the other trailers from the rodeo had set. It looked impossible.

"I don't see how looking around here is going to help find my...our horses," she said, amending the statement with a glance at Trip. She was still adjusting her thought process to their being partners on the rough stock.

Both men glanced up from where they were studying the ground and she suddenly hated that she had voiced her negative thoughts. But there were so many tracks and boots in this area.

She kept her gaze off of Trip and focused on Sean.

He gave her a reassuring smile. "I get where you're coming from, Lori. But we need to start here. It just happened last night and, it was nice that we had a short drizzle during the day yesterday so that we have all these tracks today. These tire tracks here aren't from your truck since it wasn't hooked up to the trailer. These must be of the truck that took your horses. That's a good thing. And despite all this foot traffic, all these boot prints are good." He moved to a cluster of boot tracks. "This is where the trailer hitch was. Whoever stood here was hooking the truck and trailer. It's a jumble but we might be able to get something usable from them." He pulled his phone out and started snapping pictures.

Trip went to stand beside Sean and she was left feeling like a negative ninny.

"There were at least two different men standing here," Trip said.

"Exactly," Sean agreed. They could be the thieves. That is a distinctive marking of the boot heel. Notice how the back of the heel is heavily worn on the outer edge."

She moved to look. "Oh, I see what you're saying."

For the first time since Trip had told her the news that her top-ranked horses were stolen she felt a glimmer of hope. "I'm sorry about being negative."

Sean looked sympathetic. "I get it. Cimarron Trouble is one of the best broncs on the circuit and the other four are right up there too. This has to be an upsetting situation for you. The WRC has had its fair share of bad luck this season but we'll help out any way we can to get your horses back."

Her gaze shifted to Trip. He gave her a small smile, his lip curving upward on one side and causing an unwanted flutter in her chest.

"We're going to find them," he assured her and then he turned away leaving her staring at his strong back as he began scanning the ground.

She watched him and then her gaze collided with Sean's. No doubt he could feel the tension between them, it hung in the area despite Trip's tight smile.

"What should I look for?" she asked Sean feeling self-conscious.

"Anything that seems worthwhile," he said and went back to looking around himself.

"How about this cigarette butt?" Trip asked from where he stood several feet away. "I know that there's a lot of cowboys who smoke but I can't place any of my men who do. Maybe this will come in handy."

Sean went to look. "Maybe so. It's not faded at all so it could be recent."

Sean pulled a plastic baggie from his pocket. He also pulled a small pair of tweezers from a small pouch he was carrying. "Good call." He picked the butt up with the tweezers and placed it in the bag and sealed it. up.

Deciding the best thing she could do was to look around herself, Lori got busy, determined to contribute rather than complain. She studied the indention of where the trailer had been. There were several footprints along the side of the trailer tires. "Maybe these belong to someone involved?"

Sean agreed. "Could be. We'll want to look at your men's boots and see if the imprints match."

"That can be arranged," Trip said.

"Until we know whether one of your men has these imprints we won't know if this is a significant break or not."

She tried to remember if one of her guys walked with a sway or leaned heavily on one leg. Anything that might mean an imprint with an awkward back heel like the print Sean had found near the hitch area. Harvey had a little weight on him, but Mike was skinny as a fence post. But like Trip had said earlier they had no reason to suspect either man of anything but carelessness.

Sean knelt down and rested his elbows on his knees, his cotton shirt stretched tight across his shoulders as he studied them. "It looks like three separate imprints. Different from the first one at the trailer hitch. There should be two imprints at the trailer hitch one of them will be your man and one set could be the horse thief's."

Sean took several more photos and Trip took some as well. "See the depth of this imprint. It's deeper than the other two which probably means he's heavier so my guess would be that we are dealing with two of a similar weight and one heavier."

Trip frowned. "Harvey's not the smallest guy. He's about six feet and over two hundred pounds I would estimate. Mike is smaller, about five nine but less than a hundred and seventy."

"We'll want their imprints," Sean said.

She looked at Trip, unease turning in her stomach. "You don't think Harvey's involved, do you? Daddy hired him years ago. I really can't imagine him being involved in this."

"Then there's nothing for him to worry about," Sean said. "We aren't accusing him of anything. But I still need to eliminate his boot imprint with this one. We're not claiming or insinuating guilt of any sort. I just need to continue my process of elimination to figure out who these prints belong to. Then we can decide whether these are clues."

She nodded getting what he was saying and tried not to feel guilty about not trusting the men who worked for her.

"Trip tells me you had dealings with rustlers a week ago?"

"Yes. So far nothing has turned up."

"Okay, I'll relay that back to my brothers when we look at all the factors."

They spent the next few minutes discussing what the agency could do and if they could help at all. "We'll just have to see," Sean said. "Until we dig deeper, we really don't know what we're dealing with. I'll head out to your ranch in the morning and do a few interviews. I'll just tell them I'm following up where the police left off. At this point, we aren't accusing anyone of anything. Maybe someone noticed something the police missed in their questioning. After that, I'll drive back to Dallas and catch my plane."

Lori nodded and met Trip's gaze. His brow hitched slightly as if questioning if she was okay with this. She wasn't okay with any of it. "That's fine. We'll be ready for you."

She just hoped that questioning her men didn't cause them to believe she didn't trust them. She already struggled to have them give her half the respect they'd given her father. She certainly didn't need to alienate them.

They were quiet as they left the arena and headed back toward the ranch. She raked a hand through her hair. Her thoughts swirled.

"I'll make sure all the men stay near the main compound in the morning so we can talk to them. It'll be good to see if anyone saw or heard anything out of the ordinary over the last few months. I'm not sure exactly what we're looking for but maybe slinging questions out is the way to uncover something. I know you're worried how the men will take this but stop worrying. It's your ranch, Lori. You have a right to answers and to ask anything you want to know. And as far as these horses go, so do I."

True, she told herself. "Still, I just took over the ranch and this isn't going to endear me to the men. I'm already the daughter of the boss."

"And for the ones who can't handle that I'll show them the door."

They'd been over this again and again. He'd fired three guys not long after she'd taken over for that very thing. They'd just not liked the fact that a twenty-seven-year-old woman was their boss.

"No, I don't want to do that again. No one has been rude like those others were. And I can't help feeling like I shouldn't have let them go."

She felt him tense. They'd been at odds over this from the beginning too. Silence held the inside of the truck captive.

"You're my boss, but you know I disagree with you on that."

And that was part of their problem…she hated being Trip Jensen's boss. Yes, they were partners in the stock contracting company but as for the ranch, she was his boss and he didn't seem to be able to forget that.

In the few months that her dad had been alive after he'd hired Trip, she'd been able to ignore how awkward this was going to be since she was almost two hundred miles away from the ranch while living in Houston. But then, her dad died, and she'd taken a leave of absence and come home to sort things out. And being his boss along with everything else in their past was not helping the tough situation she faced of picking up the pieces.

Trip's grip on the steering wheel tightened as regrets pounded him like baseball-sized hail. He fought hard not to overstep his boundaries, reminding himself that he was only the foreman, the manager. He was not Lori's keeper. As much as he wanted to be more to her, he wasn't. And he had to keep reminding himself of that fact. It got harder with every passing day they worked together.

"Do you really think that they'll find anything?"

"They have a great reputation so they're the best shot we have and that's why I called them."

"That was a good call. I hope we get this figured out soon." She grew quiet and nodded then went back to watching the pastures pass by.

He glanced at her profile. She looked tense. Before he could let the boss/employee relationship stop him he reached out and took her hand. "It's going to be alright," he assured her.

She met his gaze with wide sea-blue eyes and for a moment she looked so vulnerable. She was no longer the freckled faced girl who'd befriended him that first day his dad had taken him to the ranch after being hired as the foreman. Trip had been ten, and she was nine. Now, in that split second, he felt like he'd been transported to old times. When she had trusted him. So long since there had been an easiness between them.

"I hope so," she said, removing her hand from his.

A band tightened around his heart. He'd been a lonesome kid when they'd moved to Ransom Springs for the new job on the ranch and they'd moved into the manager's house. Lori had been a skinny, freckled-faced girl with pigtails and that first day she'd been wearing a pink shirt with blue jeans tucked into pink boots. Lori Calhoun had been one sassy little girl. He almost smiled remembering how she'd marched over to him as he got out of the truck.

"You know how to ride?" she'd asked looking at him skeptically.

He'd been highly offended. "Of course, I can ride," he'd boasted and she'd grinned wide, exposing a missing a tooth.

"Not as good as me," she'd said. "Come on let's saddle up."

And from that day forward they were friends. And she'd been right, that scrawny girl could ride a horse better than most grown men. Her daddy had taught her well.

They'd grown up together on the ranch and been the best of friends as kids. They'd ridden every inch of the ranch together, climbed the hills and followed the trails herding cattle and chasing strays. That had been when life was simple.

When she was about sixteen and he was just about to turn seventeen, he knew she was the girl for him. And that was when things got complicated.

His dad had taken him aside and pointed out the facts of life as far as their family was concerned—Lori was the boss's daughter and Trip was the manager's son. She would always own the ranch and he worked the ranch. And that was an impasse that he didn't need to cross. His dad also pointed out that if Trip dated Lori, and they broke up, it could put his management job in jeopardy.

A weight had settled on Trip's shoulders and on his heart at that moment. And it had changed the course of his and Lori's relationship. He'd backed away his senior year, knowing he had to. He had nothing to offer her. Nothing. And so he'd graduated and taken a job on a ranch near Texas A&M and worked hard to help put himself through college. Then he went to work right out of college selling a top brand feed and hit the road. He saved every penny he could, stocking it away for his future.

He hadn't loved his job, but the pay was good and the commissions even better. He'd dated some, but Lori had stayed on his heart. He'd tried not to care when he got word she was in a serious relationship in Houston. Tried not to care when he'd heard her relationship had fallen through. And he'd tried not to care the day her daddy had called him and offered him the ranch manager job after Trip's own daddy had announced he was retiring.

Trip had refused the offer to come back and take over where his dad had left off. The pay had been great, the opportunity undeniable—if a man wanted to manage someone else's ranch. None of that would help Trip own his own ranch or win the woman of his dreams.

When Lori's dad had called back being open about wanting to ensure the ranch was in good shape for Lori if something were to happen to him, Trip had understood where Ray was coming from. But being foreman still left him in the same position he'd always been in where Lori was concerned. As if he understood Trip's dilemma, Ray had counter-offered with the manager's job plus the opportunity to buy in as half owner of the rough stock contracting company.

Trip had taken the deal.

He'd sunk his savings into the offer and now, his future rode on the success of the rough stock business. If he could help grow the business and build it, then he could let his feelings for Lori be known.

It was getting tougher to keep them hidden with every day he was here.

He needed to know where they stood and he needed to get past the barrier of polite professionalism that was wedged between them.

CHAPTER THREE

The next day Sean showed up to the ranch and began interviewing the two men who had lost their trailer. Just like Lori feared, Harvey took offense to being questioned by Sean.

"I already answered questions for the police. Now you've hired a private eye to investigate me? Your daddy always trusted me."

She started to say something but Trip beat her to it.

"Harvey, we're not accusing you of anything but carelessness, which you and I both know Ray would not have stood for so stop with the guilt trip and answer Sean Knight's questions. We're just looking for leads." The two men stared at each other and Lori knew what Trip had said about her daddy was true.

"Fine," Harvey grunted and then glared at Sean.

Sean had remained neutral in the conflict as if he was used to this sort of thing. Lori wasn't. But she had to admit now that Harvey had been so disagreeable she was determined that he would answer the questions even if she was the one who ended up asking them.

Sean looked at Harvey's boots. It was logical that one set of prints near the hitch would be his. It wasn't the pair with the uneven heel. Harvey's had a little normal wear, but he didn't have an exaggerated worn edge like the one at the scene.

After an irritated, but somewhat cooperative Harvey left and they called in Mike. He also had a worn-down boot heel.

"Did you see anything that might get your suspicions up?" Sean asked him.

"I'm afraid not. There was nobody around while I was there it was just me. We loaded the horses up and I locked the trailer up. Then we went and got the truck."

"And it took two of you to get the truck?"

"Um, well," he hedged. "I didn't think anything about leaving the horses there. Most everyone was packing up and heading out. We see the same people at every rodeo. It never occurred to us someone would do this."

He'd only been working for the ranch for six months, hired right after Trip fired the three who hadn't liked the idea of a female boss.

Sean looked at the two of them when he'd finished the interviews. They'd found a couple of their ranch hands who had a boot heel that could possibly be a match to the one near the trailer hitch.

"So far all we have several cowboys with slanted

boot heels," Sean said.

"And there are a lot of bowlegged cowboys out there with slanted boot heels," Lori said with a sigh.

"But still, we have a cigarette butt and a slanted boot heel and when we get a break, one of those could be the ace in our pocket," Sean added. "I've got to head out if I'm going to catch my flight. We'll see you in Fort Worth. Call if you have more information. I'll do some digging and some background checks on the men working here if you'll send me the list of names. Something about all of this still doesn't feel right."

"I can do that," Trip said as they stood and headed out of the office.

Sean looked around. "So, you own the ranch," he said to Lori. "And you both own the stock contracting business? I'm not convinced this is WRC related. Those cattle being stolen could be connected to your horses being stolen."

"Yes," Lori said. "We've been thinking that too."

They stopped at Sean's truck. "So, my advice is to be on your watch and I hate to say it but don't trust anyone."

Trip met her gaze. Did Sean mean each other?

Sean's truck disappeared in a cloud of dust but his words hung in the air around Trip and Lori. He turned to her. "Do you trust me?"

She squinted at him in the sunlight as she pushed her dark hair behind her ear. "We might have our differences- the truth is, Sean could have told me straight up that you were stealing from me and I wouldn't have believed him. He was talking about everyone else working for us."

Relief washed through Trip and he fought down the need to smile. Instead, he met her serious gaze with a nod. "Okay then, that means a lot."

"So where do we go from here?" she asked, holding his gaze.

Her words brought up a whole host of wishful thinking on his part. "Want to take a walk and look at the stock heading to Fort Worth?" He needed to move.

"Sure." She fell into step with him as he walked.

"We need to do whatever it takes to figure this out," he said. "And I think you should know, that while I don't like the idea of this being an inside job like Sean implied, I'm not discounting it. Your daddy hired me because he knew he could trust me with all the things he cared about." They reached the holding pen and he met her gaze. "We came to an understanding because we had a common goal."

"Are you talking about me?" Lori asked.

At Trip's words and the look in his pale blue eyes, a shiver of awareness raced through Lori. His gaze rested on her lips then lifted to meet her eyes.

"What else would I be talking about, Lori?" he asked, his voice roughening.

Her skin tingled, she swallowed hard. Suddenly, she needed to change the subject. It was getting too close to something she didn't want to acknowledge, something she was scared to acknowledge for fear that once again her hopes and dreams would be dashed and her heart broken.

She moved a step away from him, fearing she'd throw herself at him and that would not do.

"Do you think my daddy had something wrong with him? I just, I just can't come to grips with the fact that he was thrown from his horse." There, she hadn't voiced that concern to anyone.

Trip was quiet, and she wasn't sure if it was because she'd changed the subject or because her question had startled him.

"No, he didn't say anything. And if he was having issues I never noticed it. Sometimes things just happen. Flukes, oddities," he said, his voice gentle. "If a horse trips, even the best horseman in the business, can have an accident."

Lori nodded and felt moisture at the corner of her eyes and she blinked hard, she would not cry. She took a shaky breath. He'd stood beside her at the funeral, as her ranch manager and she'd longed for her friend…

But she'd lost him when she'd pushed for their relationship to be more during the end of her junior year. He'd pulled away almost instantly and distanced himself then left for college and broke her heart.

Now, despite fighting her feelings for him and all the conflicting complicated emotions she was facing right now she would settle for just having her friend back.

But it wasn't that simple.

Anger spiked through her suddenly. She'd had her daddy's death to deal with, a ranch to sort out and in all of that, she was being forced to fight these unwanted emotions over Trip.

Her horses and cattle going missing was not helping. She'd let her defenses down because until now, they'd dealt strictly over business.

"You're right. I just can't imagine him being thrown from a horse." She took a step back from Trip. "I need to call the insurance company about filing a claim on the horses," she said, stepping back another step and fighting for calm.

He looked conflicted but just nodded curtly in agreement. She fought the want to throw herself into his arms and cry on his chest. She wouldn't let herself do that, instead, she spun and hurried toward the house, trying hard not to run.

Trip held himself stiffly where he stood and watched her hurry toward the ranch house. He rubbed the back of his neck and wondered at the wisdom of taking this job. But then, he understood why Ray had wanted him here, why he'd even been willing to sell half the stock contracting business to Trip. He wanted Lori safe and so did Trip. But he wondered if their decision was fair to Lori?

For a brief moment, it had felt like old times, when they'd been friends and confided everything to each other. And then she'd back stepped.

Torn with what to do he headed toward his truck. He had a bull to look at and he needed to put a little distance between him and Lori for a little while.

She'd probably thank him.

CHAPTER FOUR

Jolene DeLeon stared at Lori in the mirror of the Fluff-n-Buff Hair Salon two days after the horses went missing. "Girl, it has been far too long since you had these nasty split ends snipped off," she drawled then leaned in so no one else in the salon could hear. "So, how's it going with your hunky foreman? Have you let bygones be bygones and opened a new chapter in your love life?"

"Jolene, I have a lot going on at the ranch. I have cattle and now horses missing."

Her old friend shrugged. "So, more excuses to cuddle up with Trip-you-are-so-fine-Jensen." She pointed her comb at Lori and her eyes narrowed. "Do not tell me you are still holding that grudge. You and that man were this close growing up…" She locked two fingers together and waggled them at Lori. "Y'all were kids. You've both been out in the world and come back home to roost and you're both still single. Let it go and see where it goes."

Lori glared at Jolene. "Has it ever occurred to you that I may not have been in to get a trim because of the harassment you gave me about Trip last time?"

"Has it ever occurred to you that I could cut six inches of your hair off in one swipe if you keep denying you still have feelings for that man. I think your daddy, God rest his hard-headed soul, knew it too. And this is his way of making the pathway clear."

"Could we change the subject, please? And are going to trim or just harass me?"

Jolene gave a coy smile. "I'll trim but I really enjoy harassing you. You get so uptight. That's how I know you still care despite all your protesting. You do know that ever since he moved back he's been a hot topic with the gals. But he has yet to ask any one of them out—though plenty of them have practically thrown themselves in front of his truck in an attempt to get his attention."

Try as she might jealousy rose inside of Lori at the thought of other women trying to win a date with Trip. "That doesn't mean anything to me except that he's busy at the ranch since Daddy died and he has too much on his mind to notice them."

"It could mean he has you on his mind. I remember the way he used to look at you in school. He practically adored you and it was not in a my-best-friend kind of way. That hot-high-school-hunk was crazy about you and even after you two had your blowup I'd catch him watching you from a distance. And believe me, girlfriend, he looked like one lovesick cowboy, the same longing looks he'd always had for you. It never made sense to me that you two split up instead of getting closer."

Lori fought down any feelings of hope her friend's words might cause. "I really need to get back to the ranch. Can you hurry?"

Jolene gave a shrug. "Okay. Relax I'll back off. You look stressed and the last thing I want to do is add to that."

"Thanks. For everything."

With a new trim and an earful of gossip, Lori stopped by the grocery store and then headed back to the ranch. It had helped to get away. She'd been trying for two days to avoid Trip and it hadn't been hard, which meant he'd been letting her avoid him or trying just as hard to avoid her, which didn't sound like Trip.

With Jolene's voice echoing in her head she headed home. Had Jolene really seen Trip staring at her with longing?

If that were so then why had he pulled back when she'd practically thrown herself at him the week before her prom. Why had he spent the rest of his time home avoiding her like the plague?

She carried her groceries inside the house and put them away then stood at the window staring out at the barn. Was he there, in his office? She'd run like a scared rabbit after their conversation at the round pens. There was just so much going on and too many emotions floating around.

She'd thought about him for the last two days. She

had horses missing and bookings on the verge of canceling if they couldn't get the stock back and what was on her mind—Trip and the way they'd once been.

Some ranch woman she was turning out to be.

Yes, she'd taken care of business, contacted the insurance company, answered all the questions from the police and was gearing up to head to Fort Worth at the end of the week. And then Oklahoma City—if they didn't cancel on her. They had a heavy schedule but now with her five best horses missing, they were in jeopardy of losing some of their contracts.

The one blessing in all of this was that the insurance claim could help with their financial loss. But she *wanted* her horses back.

She wanted a lot of things, Trip Jensen for starters and it was driving her crazy. She so wanted to end this roller coaster of emotions that Trip had her on.

She needed to stop hiding out from him. With that on her mind, she walked to the barn. Maybe a ride would do her good. The men were sorting cattle today, maybe she'd ride out there and help. A ride sounded good, and it had been a long time since she'd cut calves from a herd.

As she entered the stable Harvey almost ran over her as he stormed out of Trip's office. His face was red with anger and the anger in his expression was vivid.

"Harvey, what's the matter?" she asked, startled by the fury in his expression.

He scowled. "I don't like people looking at me like I did something wrong." He glared at her and something inside her snapped.

She'd had enough. "No one has accused you of anything, but we had a right to ask questions." She met his stare straight on. "Sean Knight simply asked you a few questions that you should have been willing and *ready* to answer. I don't understand why you're so upset, and quite frankly, I'm about fed up with it," she said, firmly feeling herself channeling her dad.

Harvey looked startled and suddenly at a loss for words. She wasn't. "You were at the rodeo and you were responsible for those animals and if you're going to continue to work here, then you need to own up to that fact. Those animals are a huge loss to this business. Answering a few questions when I'm out five prize rodeo stock is not too much to be asked. You should have expected questions."

They stared at each other, her temper wasn't usually so quick but really, what was Harvey thinking? That they were just supposed to let her—*their* animals disappear and not ask any questions. Behind him, she saw Trip come to the door of his office.

"I guess you're right," Harvey muttered.

"I know I'm right." She couldn't help it. Over Harvey's shoulder, she saw Trip lean against the doorframe as he relaxed against it, crossed his arms and watched quietly. Supporting her but not intruding unless she needed him.

Her insides quivered. She focused on Harvey.

"Yes, ma'am," he grunted. "But I got a feeling that

nobody trusts me around here. Even though I have been here all these years. Your daddy would've trusted me."

Guilt hit her, but she quickly dismissed it. "Yes, he would have. He hired you a long time ago Harvey. But that doesn't mean he would have let you get by without answering some questions and you know it."

It hit her then that maybe Harvey might have thought he would move into the foreman position when Trip's dad had retired. Instead, her dad had brought in Trip.

Could he have been involved—*no* she wasn't going to think that. She actually trusted Harvey though she was disappointed in his response to this situation.

"This will pass, Harvey," she said. "But until it does questions might be asked. We're just trying to get to the bottom of this."

Her words didn't make him look any happier. "Fine," he grunted and walked off.

She watched him go then looked at Trip. He hitched an eyebrow then backed into his office and she followed him inside and closed the door behind her.

"So, what exactly did you say to Harvey that had him so upset?" she asked.

Trip leaned on the edge of his desk and crossed his own arms as he studied her.

"I just asked him if he remembered anything since being interviewed about the incident and why he loaded the horses before hooking the truck to the trailer. Nothing he should have gotten all huffed up about."

She sighed, letting her breath out slowly. "You're

right. But he's been here for years. I can't believe he'd be a part of stealing them. I'm not ready to believe the worst, not until we have more facts. I just won't jump to conclusions. Harvey feels like we're accusing him of something and I'm—*we're* not. Still, we have to keep an open mind and someone did this. I'm not trusting anybody except you and me."

"You're thinking what I'm thinking. And Harvey has no right to accuse us of anything."

She nodded, glad to have his support. It felt good knowing she had his backing. "I'm going to Fort Worth with you. I'm going to be on watch and have my eyes and ears open too."

"I think that's a good idea. It'll be nice to have you around."

She ran a hand through her hair. "I'm going for a ride. I need to get out in the open for a little while."

"You holding up okay?" he asked his gaze penetrating.

She shrugged. "I'm doing the best I can. This on top of Daddy only being dead five months…" she hesitated, considering her words. She'd been trying so hard to be strong.

"You want some company on your ride?" he asked.

Her pulse sped up—once the two of them had ridden everywhere on the ranch together. "Sure, just like old times," she said, trying to keep herself neutral. "But, I don't want to talk about all this. I haven't slept much and I just want a break for a few minutes. I just want a ride.

Can you do that?"

His lip hitched up on the side." I can do that because I'm in total agreement with you that you need a break. And you need some sleep. Maybe if we ride your mind will relax a bit. And I'd love to show you some of the changes we've done since you rode the ranch. Your dad was always making improvements. Of course, by truck you could see more but there are a few things to see close enough for a ride."

"That's a great idea. We can give it our best shot, anyway." She took a deep breath feeling a sense of exhilaration at the thought of riding with him, her old friend, she reminded herself. It wasn't safe to think of him as anything else. He'd made it perfectly clear that they had a professional relationship these days.

His grin though, made it a hard thing to remember. They headed into the stable. She picked a pretty mare she'd ridden in the arena a few times since she'd been home and he grabbed his black gelding. They brushed them down and saddled them and then headed out toward the horizon. The simple act of leaving the house and ranch compound behind gave her a sense of relief from her shoulders. The wind was light but the fresh air scented lightly with mixtures of clover and honeysuckle lifted her spirits.

"When's the last time you rode out here?" he asked.

She glanced at him. He looked so good in the saddle, always had. Trip was just the epitome of the perfect cowboy. His hat sat low over his brow, his back was straight and he moved with the horse in a smooth, easy way. He fit out here in every way. Her heart longed for what could have been, for what she'd hoped could be at one time. She looked away and concentrated on what he'd asked.

"It's been too long. I was here, you know the month before Daddy died. I thank God every day that I came home that weekend. I'd needed to come home but work was busy and…well he and I had had a fight. I came home anyway finally and…" She paused, realizing she was rambling and hadn't answered his question. "I didn't take time to ride that weekend. And since I've been home, well, you know, I've been busy going over the books and trying to get a hold on the business. The few times I've ridden in the round pen are all I've taken time for."

She shot him an embarrassed glance, and he nodded. She felt so guilty for having not come home.

"You said you didn't want to talk about the horse theft but do you want to talk about anything else? Like why you were mad at your dad? None of my business I know, but I'm here if you need a sounding board. I seem to remember we used to do that pretty well for each other."

Her heart cinched tight, she swallowed hard as her throat suddenly ached with the want to talk like old times. She rested her wrist on the saddle horn and held the reins lightly with her fingers and tried to relax, letting the feel of the horse's walk ease through her. But she was so wound up it was hard to let go.

"I struggle," she admitted at last. "Struggle with the fact that I wasn't here. And that he died thinking I was never coming home to live on the ranch he'd built for me."

At her revelation Trip pulled his horse to a halt, and she did the same.

"Never? You don't plan to make Calhoun Ranch your home—*ever*? I don't get that?"

She looked down. "I'm not sure anymore. I'm dealing with a lot right now."

And she was. Part of that involved Trip. But she couldn't tell him that.

CHAPTER FIVE

Trip had noticed she hadn't been around but once between the time he'd started working and Ray had died. His own father had told him that Ray and Lori had had an argument but that Ray had been very closed mouth about it but it had hit him hard. By the time Trip had agreed to work for Ray the rancher had seemed set on his plan of action where Trip was concerned but he'd never realized that Ray was actually setting him up to run the ranch because Lori had no plans to ever take control.

The idea was hard-hitting and wrong. He stared at her. "I don't get this. You always wanted to run this ranch. You and your dad talked about it for as long as I can remember. What happened?" Maybe he shouldn't ask but he couldn't help it.

"Things…change. Daddy said he wanted me to stretch my wings and try new things. He said it would be good for me and so I went. But then he decided when he wanted me to come back home. But I had commitments.

And I enjoyed working with the marketing firm and I wasn't ready. He took that as I was never coming home and he put pressure on me. I rebelled." She shifted in the saddle, it creaked with the movement. "I'm very much like him, you know, stubborn and hard-headed as they come and independent. And so, he pushed my buttons, and I buried my feet in the dirt and took a stance like a stubborn horse determined not to budge for the trainer. I was okay about coming home on my terms but not to be ruled and led by Daddy. I loved him so much but I got scared that he wanted to control too much of my life. I stayed away."

He could understand her thinking. Ray was strong-willed, but he was right, so was she. It would be hard not for them to clash, eventually. But—"I'm actually shocked you planned to stay away even if you and your dad fought. I never thought you would do anything but come back to the ranch. I mean, your dad told me you planned to stay at your job in marketing a little longer but I didn't think…" he paused then added, "I don't think he believed you wouldn't be back."

She blinked, and he saw the tears before she dashed them away with her fingertips. She seemed to always be close to tears these days and her daddy had been gone five months. She was beginning to believe things were never going to get better.

"I know," she said, hearing the slight crack in her

voice. "And then he'd hired you a few months before and demanded that I come home that weekend. Thankfully, I did, and he explained what he was doing. But, I had no idea a month later he'd be gone."

She urged her horse to start moving again and Trip did too. They were approaching the gate, and he moved ahead of her to lean down and opened it from the saddle. They rode through and he held back then closed it. She used the time to collect her emotions. She was a strong, independent woman she needed to start acting like it.

Very troubled, Trip rode back and closed the gate again and then loped to where she was. She glanced over her shoulder at him as he approached and then she nudged her horse into a trot and then they took off at a gallop.

Trip laughed and took out after her. She needed this. There was freedom galloping across an open pasture especially when you were feeling hemmed in or down and Lori had to be feeling both.

Bluebonnets were blooming as they raced over a hill of them and down the slope toward a gurgling creek that wove through the ranch. In their early years, they raced this path many times and Lori and her horse always jumped the creek to the other side. He wondered if she'd do it now. He wondered how long it had been since she'd let herself run truly free like this.

He watched as she made her approach and knew the mare she was riding could make it. When she leaned low and didn't slow down he knew she was going for it. She rode the horse as effortlessly as she'd always ridden and easily jumped the water. When her horse landed Lori stayed in the saddle perfectly and guided her horse back to face him. She was smiling brilliantly and nearly knocked him out of his saddle, she was so beautiful and happy looking. He urged his gelding forward and took the leap, felt the power of the horse as it sprang forward and sailed easily to the other side. Laughing, he pulled up and his horse pranced a bit as it settled down.

"You couldn't resist," he said, smiling.

Her eyes were flashing with happiness. "I know, I couldn't. It just felt good."

He dismounted, and she did the same to allow their horses to get a drink from the clear creek. It was an old routine they'd done so many times growing up together when things had been good between them. He let go of the reins knowing Jep and Bell weren't going anywhere.

The mesquite trees and the oaks were thick further down the creek but here the land was clear and perfect for enjoying a picnic or fishing. Or, as they'd done many times, wading in the shallow water.

"Are you going to pull off your boots and roll up your pants for a wade in the creek?" he asked.

She placed her hands on her hips and thought about it. "No, not today I don't think. But, maybe another day."

He moved to stand beside her and they watched the horses enjoy the water.

"So, there will be another time? Are you planning to

stay?"

"We used to love coming here," she said, her voice smiling.

"Yes, we did." He didn't tell her that there wasn't a time that he rode by this spot that he didn't think of her.

She smiled. "I remember when I was about eleven, you fell in."

"I was twelve, and you pushed me in." He scowled, then laughed.

"Oh, is that what happened," she teased. "I don't seem to recall it that same way."

He grunted. "Recall it however you want but you pushed me that day." He laughed, knowing full well that she knew exactly what had happened that day.

"If you say so. But I'll never admit that."

"I know."

"But you got me back," she accused. "I came in to help you up and you pulled me in."

He grinned, remembering. "You jumped up faster than a jackrabbit running from a rattlesnake. You were drenched and laughing…" And beautiful. His heart swelled because that had been the first time he'd noticed his friend as more. That had been the beginning for him, an adolescent longing for more and too scared to let her know it. "I've missed you, Lori," he said, unable to stop the admission.

She inhaled slowly. "I've missed you too. We were a good pair back then."

"I think your dad knew we'd be a good pair again."

She looked at him then, and something sparked in her eyes. Something that sent his pulse careening. As quick as the heated gaze met his, she extinguished the flame and hid it behind blank eyes.

"Why did you pull away from me your senior year? You just closed me out. And then you left."

And there it was. The question that hung between them that she'd never asked, the question he'd tried to avoid.

"You were the boss's daughter. I was the manager's son. And—" He halted, uncertain if this was the right move to make but certain it was time to be open with her. "As kids that was fine but then we weren't kids anymore."

She startled him when she stepped toward him, her expression confused. "I was always your friend no matter what. I made a mistake letting you know I cared for you that night. If I'd have known my admission was going to drive you away, I wouldn't have said anything. I never dreamed you would turn away from me."

"I'm sorry, Lori."

Her eyes filled with pain. "You walked away and found new friends and left me hanging. And then you left for college and barely acknowledged me before you left."

"We don't need to open this up." He had wanted so many times to let his guard down with her, to step back across the line he'd drawn in the dirt between them after his dad had told him that his manager's job could be in jeopardy if Trip got romantically involved with Lori.

Going away to school had been the right excuse.

"No, I think now is a good time to open it up." She lifted her chin stubbornly. "I'm about done, I think, with unanswered questions. I cared for you and you shunned me. It hurt and I think I deserve to know."

It took everything he had in him not to reach for her. She was only a step away from him and the fierce hurt mingled with fire and accusation pushed him to his limits. "I never meant to hurt you. I did what I had to do."

"Too bad, you did hurt me. I cared for you," she gritted out.

"I cared for you too. Lori, you were the boss's daughter. I had nothing to offer you."

She recoiled as if he'd slapped her. His heart thundered. "You had everything to offer me."

"What? I owned nothing, you owned a ranch. I was the ranch hand. Do you know what people would have said if I'd dared to be more than your friend? They'd have said I was trying to move up in the world by using you."

Her jaw locked in place and her eyes glittered. "You walked away and closed me out so people wouldn't talk? People are always going to talk and I couldn't care less."

"But I couldn't let them talk about that. I couldn't be that guy. And then there was the fact that my dad was afraid if I let my feelings be known and we broke up his job could have been on the line."

She laughed. "Daddy wouldn't have done that. And neither would I."

"It wouldn't have worked."

"Funny, I never took you for a coward."

He sucked in a sharp breath. "I'm not a coward. I did what I had to do."

"Oh really, so you just assumed if we, you and I, explored the feelings we had for each other outside of being friends that we wouldn't make it. And that I would think less of you because my daddy had a ranch."

"A ranch that was going to be yours."

She glared at him. "In my heart of hearts, I knew that was why you pulled away from me." She swung around and strode to her horse. In one swift movement, she swept up the reins, grabbed the saddle horn and stepped into the stirrup then settled into the saddle.

"This ranch turned into a deficit to me after you left. It cost me you and now it's cost me, my dad," her voice broke. She tore her eyes off him and glared at the surrounding beauty, a frown hardened her face. "It's too much."

He watched as she rode her horse through the stream up the shallow bank and then sent the horse into a gallop back toward home.

Trip didn't move. Couldn't move. He just watched her ride away.

Was he a coward?

Had he taken everyone's reactions for granted because his dad had?

And what was holding him back now?

CHAPTER SIX

Anger drove Lori to ride straight home and not look back. She didn't care if Trip followed or not. She'd pushed the anger at him deep, she had to or it would have driven her crazy. She hadn't even acknowledged until that moment that she'd resented the ranch. Oh, she'd felt it after Trip had pulled away because she'd known that had to be part of it. She had ears and she'd heard other boys tease him, that he should grow up and marry her because she and the ranch were a package deal. But he'd just been her friend and had told them to lay off.

But in the end, the digs had hit their target.

And deny it all she wanted but she and the ranch were a package deal. And the ranch was worth a lot…enough to run a man like Trip off.

She'd handed her horse over to one of the ranch hands as soon as she got back to the stable and headed to the house. She did not want to talk to Trip anymore today.

The office phone was ringing as she entered, jolting

her from her thoughts. Glad for the distraction she grabbed the phone from its dock and answered it immediately.

"Lori, this is Madge Clark, the secretary at the Oklahoma Buckout Rodeo. I need to have a word with you."

Dread filled her. "Sure, what can I do for you?" She'd been waiting for this call.

The Buckout had specifically booked her top five horses. And they were missing. She'd wondered how long she'd have before they'd hear the news and call. Obviously, word was out.

Madge didn't waste time. "As you know our event is with the top-ranked saddle broncs. And well, we've heard Cimarron Trouble and your other top four horses are missing. Have you got any news on them?"

"None so far. We've got the Knight Investigation Agency looking into it as well as the TSCRA because we've also had some cattle stolen."

"Good. If anyone can locate them those two agencies can. Do you have any leads? We hate this for you. But as much as I hate it, if your top five can't show up then we have to bring in the next in rank to fill in."

Lori rubbed her temple, feeling a headache coming on. Her entire body tensed. "In all honesty, Madge, we have no leads at this point. We don't even have a motive other than what they're worth. But they're branded and it will sure be hard for them to be sold. So, it's going to be hard for someone to get by with this as far as I can see."

"I think so too. But if they aren't found then I'll have to let Stan Kramer's stock fill the slots since they rank above your other horses. And that's how we do this event."

Lori's heart sank. This was what she'd feared. To make it to the finals her horses needed this rodeo. "Can you give me at least until after Fort Worth before you cancel?"

"We can do that. And I wish you the best of luck. I'll contact you soon after Fort Worth."

Lori leaned her head back against her dad's chair and closed her eyes. "Okay, fair enough." They ended the call and Lori pushed out of the chair and paced the office.

She stopped to stare out the window and saw Trip heading to his truck. She needed to tell him the news but not right now. She just couldn't handle facing him again today. Not after having lost it out there like she'd done.

No matter what was between them they were going to have to run the ranch together or she was going to need to go back to Houston and frankly she no longer knew what it was she wanted to do.

But for tonight she was going to relax in a warm bath listen to a book on tape and try really hard to escape everything around her for a few hours. And if she was lucky she'd sleep and wake up ready to face another day.

The morning after their fight Trip, tired and in a less than happy mood from lack of sleep and concern over the way things were going, headed to see Lori. His men had quickly gotten out of his way and headed off to their various jobs for the day, including Harvey. The man was irritating and obviously was looking for ways to lose his job. Trip hadn't figured out why the man was still here but he was watching him. And he wasn't firing him, not yet anyway.

Mike, on the other hand, continued to apologize for leaving the trailer and the kid was working harder than everyone else trying to keep his job. Trip figured he'd just done what he was told to do the night the trailer load of horses was stolen.

Trip's friend, Vance Presley had called this morning and said they'd had rustlers on their pastures that bordered Lori's ranch. Trip had made a decision as he'd hung the phone up and was heading to find Lori. They might have their problems but he was still her foreman and needed to do his job. He was walking out of the stables when he saw Lori come out of the house. His gut clenched as she came his way.

Yesterday he'd hurt for her and he hurt for the pain he'd put her through. But he didn't, in all good conscience, believe now was the time to place any other kind of pressure on her by hashing out their past and their future. Any hope of getting past her resentment she felt about everything had been hit hard yesterday. He'd left her alone after their ride, deciding they both needed time to pull back despite every fiber of his being wanting to go after her.

"I have news," she said halting at the tailgate of his truck. Keeping distance between them.

She looked weary as if she hadn't slept either. "What's happened?"

"I got a call about the Buckout. If we can't recover our horses within a few days after Fort Worth is over they're going to give the contract to Ray Kramer."

He grimaced. "I was afraid of this. If Kramer wasn't such a jerk I wouldn't mind it so much but the guy is a jerk."

"How do you mean? I don't know him. He must have come on the scene while I was away."

"Let's just say he's not my favorite person. We're going to find your horses," he said, more determined than ever to get them back.

"Our horses. You are just as much an owner as I am."

He nodded, seeing the impersonal glint in her eyes and not liking it at all. He wanted to see that spark of connection that was usually there, despite her fight not to let it show. This morning the light was out and it disturbed him more than anything. But clearly, she was trying, like he was, to get back to the impersonal footing they'd been teetering on before the ride yesterday.

"Yeah, I know. We're going to find them. I wanted to run an idea by you. I'm not willing to trust anyone who works here at the moment and decided to let the Presleys in on what's going on. I think we need some extra ears at Fort Worth. And frankly, around here too. Your dad hired me to look out for your interests and that's what I plan to do. That being said, I want to bring Vance and his family into the fold on this. If you agree."

If there was anyone he knew he could trust it was Vance and his dad and four brothers. Marcus, the father had been Ray Calhoun's best friend. He would have trusted them too.

"Sure, I trust them completely. I'm actually startled Marcus hasn't called to check on me but I think they were in Florida last week for Lana's wedding so they've been busy."

"Yes, that's where they were but they're home. And Vance called and said they had cattle stolen out of the pastures sharing a fence with you. I thought I'd ride over there and talk to them about it. About all of it."

"Rustlers—I'm sick of them," she snapped, her pretty face twisting with disgust. "What do you have in mind? I'm all in and going over there with you."

Trip hated this. For a moment in time yesterday they'd almost turned back time to the way they'd once been. He wanted that back…

He just wasn't sure there was any way to ever get back there again.

For now, he had a job to do.

CHAPTER SEVEN

Lori struggled to remain unaffected by Trip. But she was. She should have been over this years ago, but she'd held it in for so long that despite everything, he had an effect on her.

"Vance is riding in the saddle bronc competition and I want to see if he'll be on the lookout and listen for anything that seems suspicious. And all of them would do anything to help you."

It was true. The Presleys had always been her neighbors. Five boys and one girl. Lana had been one of her friends growing up and had just married. The guys, as far as she knew, were all still single and running the ranch.

"Do you want to head over there now and see who is around?"

"Sure." They climbed into the truck and she could feel Trip slide a glance her way several times as he drove. He was not going to bring up their fight from the day before. She wasn't either, she was going to let it ride and sink back into the dark.

Vance and Drake were the first Presleys they saw as they drove up to the arenas. They were looking over a group of horses in the round pen.

"Hey little girl," Drake said, grinning with that slightly crooked smile and twinkling eyes.

She laughed as he gave her a big hug. They'd seen each other several times since she'd been home, always offering her any help she needed. Drake was the oldest of the kids and had always liked to tease her and Lana. Who was she kidding, they all teased her and Lana.

"You look tired," Vance said, studying her as he gave her a quick hug.

"I'm fine," she said, glancing at Trip. "How was Lana's wedding?"

Drake looked pleased. "It was great. Lana will be moving back to Texas after the honeymoon so we're very happy about that."

"Cam's got a ranch over toward Henderson," Vance added. "And he's a good guy. His family owns the resort on the Windswept Bay. It was nice. Not that I'm into the beach myself, but Lana liked it."

Cooper strode up and overheard the conversation. "But we're glad she met a cowboy who is bringing her back to Texas. That place is beautiful but Lana belongs in Texas." He grinned and then also gave Lori a quick hug. "Good to see you, stranger."

"Stranger? I saw you last week at the diner having

dinner with a pretty blonde."

He grinned. "Well, you won't marry me so I have to keep looking."

She laughed. "Right."

Cooper was a flirt. He shot Trip a look. "You need to take Lori to that new place in town. It's nice and the food is great."

Trip met her gaze and her insides warmed. "Maybe I'll do that," he said, startling her. "But first, we came to ask for your help. Did you hear Lori had her top-ranked horses taken from the Mesquite rodeo? I figure news is just starting to get out but y'all were busy with the wedding and all."

"Do what?" Vance growled.

"Who? This rustling is out of hand," Cooper snapped.

Brice rode up on his horse just in time to hear what was said. "No kidding," he said his serious gaze blazing.

Shane was quiet as his brothers digested the news. "We had a load go missing while we were gone. We were just about to address the problem. You had a load go missing last week, right? And now these horses. I've called TSCRA and alerted them."

"We've done it too. And the Knight Investigation Agency is looking into the horses since it happened at a WRC sanctioned rodeo."

"Do you think they're related incidents?" Vance was the first to ask.

Trip shrugged. "We're waiting on an update from them today. But I'm not sure if the two are related or not.

The deal is, we don't know who to trust. It could be an inside job from someone on the ranch as it often is. Or your ranch. And then the rodeo, so who knows. We don't want to accuse the two men who were responsible for the trailer of horses but Sean Knight is suspicious. He's the brother who came out the day after it happened and looked around and asked questions. It could also be personal because we let some men go when Lori took over the ranch."

Drake stared hard from one to the other. "So what do you plan to do? And what do we need to do?"

"Right," Cooper said. "Whatever you need we're here to help."

Five, tough cowboys stepped forward to flank Trip and six pairs of eyes focused on Lori. Her knees went weak at the powerful show of support.

"There you go," Trip said. "Your own posse."

Marcus Presley's black Dodge truck drove up the lane and crossed the gravel yard to come to a halt in front of them. Marcus climbed out and strode toward them. Clearly concerned as he looked at the group. "What's up? Lori, I just got a call from a friend who told me you had horses stolen in Mesquite?"

"And leave it to Dad to be the one who hears the news," Drake said, giving a dry laugh.

Marcus hugged her and looked down at her before he let her go. "Have you come to let us in on this, darlin'?" he asked. "Because you know we're not going to stand for this."

"Thanks, Marcus. Yes, we've been telling the guys about it. And we're about to get together a plan of action."

He let her go. "Good, glad I got here when I did."

Trip filled Marcus in and then looked at Vance. "You'll be in Fort Worth riding in the saddle broncs and I was hoping that you could keep your ears open for anyone saying anything that might seem suspicious.

"You'll know what to look for, just anything out of place. If you notice anybody slipping around back there or trailers, maybe that shouldn't be there. We don't know that someone isn't going to steal someone else's stock. This might not be only targeted at Lori."

"True," Drake agreed.

If I think anything is off I'll say so," Vance said quickly. "I'm all in."

His brothers echoed his sentiment.

"I think we can all make the rodeo under the guise of watching Vance compete," Marcus said. "But the reality is we'll be mingling and asking questions."

"Let's do it," Cooper said and all his brothers agreed.

Lori was overwhelmed again by their support. "You guys are going to make me cry, I mean this is just too much to ask."

Trip put his arm around her and pulled her into his side giving her a gentle hug. His action touched her deeply and made their fight the day before seem small.

Drake smiled. "That's what friends are for, you know?"

"Yes, and I'm so blessed to have all of you. Daddy is smiling right now I'm sure."

Marcus grinned. "He'd be haunting us if we weren't helping you."

"You're probably right." She laughed as did everyone, knowing her dad had been so strong-willed it fit his personality. She missed him so much but felt him there with her, surrounded by this wonderful support network of friends.

With a plan of attack, she and Trip headed home.

"You're not alone," Trip said, quietly as they started driving.

"I know." She had good neighbors and friends and it helped to know that she had all those strong, great cowboys with her. "Thank you, Trip. We have some past that we need to let go of, I agree. But Daddy knew what he was doing when he worked so hard to hire you back on as manager. I'm sorry I was so mad yesterday."

He took his right hand off the steering wheel and took her hand but kept his eyes straight ahead as he drove.

"The reality is you had a right to be." He slowed the truck on the quiet country road and turned to face her. "Lori, I'm sorry. We're complicated, I'll admit that, but you need to know I'm here for you, just like the Presleys are. I can't guarantee you'll get your horses back before Oklahoma, but if they're still alive and breathing out there, we will find them. I promise."

She believed him. His words meant a lot. "I think so too. Thank you." His hand on hers felt so good. Since her dad died she'd felt alone and distant, now she didn't.

She turned her hand over so that their palms touched. She wrapped her fingers around his and squeezed tightly. He squeezed back and butterflies lifted and fluttered through her chest taking light to all the dark corners of her heart.

And it scared her to death…because it was opened up to being broken again.

They made it to the ranch and Trip's heart was racing and it was all he could do not to pull Lori into his arms and kiss her like he'd always dreamed of doing. But he didn't need to do that right now. She just needed him to do his job and be there for her. She was still adjusting to losing her dad. And then losing the cattle and horses on top of that. She had too many things to deal with right now. But that didn't make it any easier on him.

His phone rang as he was pulling to a stop in front of the house. "It's Jesse Knight. He's the last one of the brothers I talked to. I'll come into the house with you so we can take this together."

She nodded and got out. He answered the call as he followed her up the walk and into the house. "Hey, Jesse. Good to hear from you." He followed Lori into the office.

"I have some news."

"Great. Lori's here with me in her office. I'll put you on speaker phone."

"That's good," Jesse said. "Hi, Lori. I think you both

might be interested in something we've dug up. Your man, Harvey once worked for Kramer Stock. Did you know that? I figure since Lori just got involved with the ranch workings again that she wouldn't know but maybe you knew, Trip?"

Trip frowned. "No, I didn't know. He was here during my dad's time as manager, but I think Ray hired him. He's been less than cooperative since the horses were stolen." Trip didn't like it. "Though we've taken precautions on the hunch, it could be an inside job I've been holding out hope that it wouldn't be."

"Me too," Lori said, looking pained by the news.

"I get that," Jesse agreed. "But this doesn't look good. Stan Kramer doesn't have the best reputation out there among other rodeo stock contractors but it's undeniable that he does have some bucking stock moving up the ranks."

"Tell me about it," Trip grunted. He'd had his run-ins with Kramer. "His horses might buck good, but I question his treatment of them. And we had a horse colic the month after I took this job. I couldn't pin on Kramer but we had suspicions about them tampering with our feed. And it just happened that his horse got to fill the spot on the ticket when we had to pull out."

Lori's eyes widened. "Did Dad suspect him of tampering with the horse feed?"

"He did. But to steal a trailer full of horses would be bold of him. Since his five automatically would fill the ticket it seems a little too bold."

"Yes," Jesse agreed. "But if he was desperate, he might do it."

Trip's adrenaline spiked. "And is he?"

"Sean, Michael and I believe he could be. We've got a source that says the bank is on his heels hard. And my wife, Carly, also has had her own run-in with the man with her stock contracting company. She's not surprised by any of this either. We've quietly opened an investigation into Kramer's dealings and wanted to let you know."

"What should we do about Harvey?" Trip asked. But his gut told him the man was too sensitive about being questioned.

"Don't do anything for now. Let us dig deeper. But it goes without saying that you need to keep your eyes open. And we will all be in Fort Worth if possible. We've got several investigations going right now but we're zeroed in on this."

"Okay, thanks, we'll see you there," Trip said.

"Thanks, Jesse. I'm grateful for your help. See you in Fort Worth." She was frowning as he ended the call. "I hate this. I know Harvey has been defensive this whole time but I still don't want to believe it. He's been here for so many years."

"Yeah, I hate it. But, my gut is telling me it isn't a coincidence. He's been testy ever since I signed on. Look, everyone is working cattle in the north section today and I need to go check on things. But then I'm going to check on the cattle in the south pastures near where the Presley's cattle went missing. We may have been hit also and not know it yet."

"I'll come with you. I'm sick of this, Trip. And I'm done feeling lost in all of this. This is my ranch and someone has a reckoning coming if they think I'm an easy mark."

Trip couldn't help smiling. He saw the spark of fire back in her eyes. "Well, well, well. Welcome home at last Lori Calhoun."

She laughed despite everything. "Thanks. This has been one evolution of a day for me. Now let's go check on the cattle. And then we'll come back and take a look at the books on our rough stock. I want to see the records on that sick horse you just told Jesse about. The one that got replaced by Kramer's horse. I know you and Daddy had plans to make our rough stock into the best program around and I want that also, Trip. Especially now."

"Especially now?" he said with a question in his voice.

Her eyes twinkled. "Now that I've decided I'm not leaving. I'm making my stake here Trip. Can you handle that?"

His heart slammed against his ribs. "I can handle it."

CHAPTER EIGHT

Later, they drove up to where the men were branding and vaccinating the herd of cattle. Before they had a chance to get out of the truck Harvey galloped over on his horse to Trip's side of the truck and glared down at him.

"Do you not think I can handle working the cattle now?"

Lori's temper shot to the sun. "What did he say," she hissed, not believing her ears. Trip reached out and put a hand on her arm. She kept silent.

"Harvey," Trip said and his hand gently squeezed her arm. "I have no doubt you can handle this, but our *boss* wanted to look at her cattle," Trip said with a calm voice edged in steel. "It has nothing to do with you. We're just here to watch for a minute. Then we're moving on."

"Right. Like I'll believe that." He whirled his horse around and galloped back to the cattle.

Trip got out of the truck and she did the same. She was fuming. "Who does he think he is?" she snapped.

"Hang on, boss," Trip chuckled. "I'm not sure what he thinks he's accomplishing but let it slide for now. I'm actually here to push his buttons. We want him to mess up. I'm not going to take his bait. I'll have my moment."

"Fine. For now. But he's not making it easy."

He winked at her. "Patience. For a few minutes and then we'll head out to the other pasture to check on the other herd."

"Okay, go for it. But I'm not feeling particularly forgiving at the moment so he better not cross me."

He chuckled. "Feisty, I like it."

Lori was hotter than she could remember ever being when they got back in the truck and headed across the pastures to the far side of the ranch. The fact that Harvey could be so belligerent and probably responsible for taking or helping steal her horses got under her skin like a hot poker. She hadn't been this angry since the year Trip pulled away from her and went another direction from their friendship and the future she'd hoped to have with him.

But she was moving on from that and pushed that aside. She could not keep going back to the past, she had to let it go and focus on the here and now. On the ranch. Harvey might very well be messing with the legacy her father built for her and also with the business that she and Trip shared. And if he wasn't the culprit, then he was not doing himself any favors with his behavior.

"You doing okay over there?" Trip asked finally. "You cooling off any. I could tell you were about to blow a gasket back there."

"Harvey has a chip on his shoulder. And it's not just about the horse trailer stock gone missing. His behavior is bizarre and I just can't take it."

Trip shot her a narrowed-eyed glance. "But you did good. We didn't need to make him think we have any suspicions. Let him be that way, I'm going to nail him if he stole those horses."

"I'm with you, just furious at the moment. I have a hunch that he thought the manager's position was his. I think he has a grudge against my dad, which would mean the ranch and me and you also because you got the job he thought my dad was going to give to him."

"I think you might be right but we will see. Soon."

"I hope so. Maybe they'll slip up and the Knights will dig up something more on them. Or who knows, maybe we'll catch them. I'm looking forward to catching them, honestly, I'm angrier about this than I've been in a very long time. I'm as mad as I was when you put distance between us and found new friends then left for college—" The words just flowed before she had time to stop them. Trip went still, his hands tightened on the steering wheel and his jaw muscle flexed with tension but he didn't look at her. Didn't say anything.

Maybe getting how angry she'd been out in the open was a good thing. Trip had had his reasons for doing what he did—which she didn't completely understand but that didn't diminish how hurt she'd been. Wounded.

Still, the little voice of reason in her head reminded her, he'd been her friend, but he'd never said he loved her. He had no obligation to her back then or now. And she needed to come to grips with that fact.

It didn't matter if she'd loved him because that fact didn't mean he had any obligation to her. None at all.

She bit her lip as the war in her head and heart waged on. She glanced at him but he was staring straight ahead and as tense as she'd ever seen him.

They'd reached the ranch boundary fence and she saw the cattle at the bottom of the hill. Trip stopped the truck and rammed the gear into park. Tension filled the cab like a thick fog. He pushed open his door and got out, slamming it behind him.

It hit her then exactly how upset he was. Maybe she'd gone too far. Heart thundering, she went after him.

CHAPTER NINE

Trip could barely think straight. He told himself to calm down but clearly Lori didn't get what he had gone through when he'd pulled away from her. He couldn't take it anymore. He strode around the front of the truck and met her. Pain was in her eyes.

"Trip, I didn't mean to bring that up agai—"

"Lori, I had nothing to offer you. It didn't mean I didn't want you…" He pulled her into his arms and saw her eyes flare wide just before he covered her mouth with his.

He heard her small gasp and then she melted into him, her arms went around him and she responded to his kiss. He loved her with a depth she had no idea about but it was true.

He felt her heart pounding against his own, felt the curve of her body against him and the softness of her lips moving beneath his… He broke the kiss, needing to pull back. "Lori, I'm warning you, when we find our horses I plan to move forward not backward. I love you, always have."

Tears filled her eyes.

"Don't cry, I don't want to ever hurt you again. I only want to make you smile."

She smiled gently. "I may never stop smiling now."

"And then I'll be a happy man." He smiled.

She kissed his lips. "I love you and thank you for opening up to me."

"I couldn't stand to see you hurting because of something I did. I just thought I needed to give you time to heal from your grief and then the cattle and horses got stolen and I didn't want to add any more stress to you. But by holding back I realized I was adding to your stress."

She laid her head against his chest. "Daddy isn't coming back. And I'm coming to terms with that and I'll always miss him. But feeling so alone was the hardest thing. And then, after I'd adjusted, somewhat, to losing you, I had to come back here and see you again. Despite feeling alone I had to work with you every day and try not be affected. It just intensified everything."

His arms tightened around her. "You're not alone, darlin'. I'm here for you. And it feels so good to have you in my arms." He rested his head against hers and they just held each other.

Lori couldn't believe she was finally in Trip's arms. That he'd told her he loved her and was promising to be in her life.

She sighed and opened her eyes, looking across the land they'd roamed together as kids. "I have so many memories of us, roaming this ranch together. It feels so right to have you here with me."

"I'm thrilled to be here with you."

Her gaze rested on the knee tall grass. "Are those tracks?" she asked, lifting her head from his chest.

"Where?"

She pointed a few feet away. Trip released her and moved to where the grass was bent down.

"Yes, it is. And I haven't had men over here for a couple of days. I think we've had unwanted visitors."

Trip's mind whirled. "I have a suspicion that someone was scouting your herd. Rustlers took cattle from the Presleys next-door and checked yours out the same night. From what Vance said they took a trailer load so probably plan to come back for these. Soon."

"We need to do a stakeout," Lori snapped, anger on her pretty face. "I'm so done with this."

He smiled, despite everything. "Me too. I am going to start spending the next few nights on stakeout watching and waiting." He strode further down the hill following the tracks through the tall weeds.

Lori trudged beside him. "Me too."

"No, you will—"

"Be right here beside you. No way am I letting you do this alone."

"I'll get one of the Presleys to join me."

"I'm doing this," she said, stubborn as ever.

"Fine. But you'll stay out of the way. I'm not letting you get hurt."

She crossed her arms. "I'm capable of taking care of myself. I'll bring my rifle."

Stubborn woman. "I'm going to call Jesse back and let him know what's going on. We better go if we're going to get ready and be back here before too late."

Now if he could just keep her safe everything would be fine.

CHAPTER TEN

It was a cloudy night as Trip parked the truck in a stand of Mesquite trees along the creek. He cut the lights and he and Lori settled in to wait.

Ever since Trip had opened up to her that afternoon and had kissed her Lori had been floating on a cloud. Now sitting in the truck with him she could hardly believe it. He'd told her he loved her. She was finding it hard to concentrate on anything other than that fact.

She waited all these years, eight years. And then all those years before that—it seemed like she had been waiting all of her life to hear Trip tell her that he loved her. And now he had.

Now they needed to get through all of this junk with the ranch, get past this rustling and find their horses and cattle and put an end to all this nonsense so that the stock company could be a success. She understood that he needed that. Trip was the kind of man who had to bring something to the table.

But she'd needed something too, needed him to open up to her like he'd done today. There was an ache inside of her that his words had soothed. His words had vanquished. The ache was gone because he *loved* her and that was the most valuable thing in the world to her. Now that she had that, she didn't care if someone came and stole every cow or horse she owned. She had everything she needed with Trip's love.

But understanding what he needed drove the fire inside of her to stay out here and wait and watch and try and catch whoever was doing this. They needed to see if the rustlers stealing the cattle were the same ones who'd taken her horses. For the sake of the ranch, the stock company, and Trip.

In the darkness, he reached out and took her hand. The thrill went through her as his warm calloused hand wrapped around hers. He interlaced his fingers with hers and there they sat.

It was midnight, and they had a busy day tomorrow as the horses would be loaded in the morning and taken the three-hour drive to Fort Worth and then the rodeo would start in the evening. They were both going to be worn out.

She yawned. "If they're coming I wish they would come now so we can find out who they are, catch them and then we can go and sleep a little. We are going to be so tired tomorrow night at the rodeo."

He chuckled. "You're right about that. I don't think either of us slept last night. You can lay down and rest your head on my thigh and sleep. I'll let you know if they show up."

She squeezed his hand. "I'm not doing that. You'd probably sneak out and leave me snoring. Besides, I'm not abandoning you here in the truck while you have to stay awake and watch."

She felt his grin in the darkness. She could barely see him since he'd cut all the dash lights off inside the truck.

"I'll be fine. You really should rest."

"And you really should remember that I'm not going to do that." As she was saying the words, she saw a light bob in the distance. "Do you see that," she hissed as if whoever was in the truck could hear her talking.

"I see it. We have company."

"How many do you think there are?" She was still talking in a hushed voice.

"I don't know, but we'll know soon enough. Whatever happens, stay behind me. I'd rather you stay in the truck, but I know that's not gonna happen."

"You *do* know me."

He gave a dry laugh. "I know you."

Before she realized what, he was doing he pulled her into his arms, cupped her face in the darkness and kissed her again. Butterflies, fireflies, and moths with fire-laced wings exploded through her chest. This kiss was different from that afternoon. It was hard and fast and almost desperate. It left her breathless when he pulled away. And wanting more.

"Lori," his voice was raspy. "I can't have anything

happen to you. Do you understand that?"

"Yes. But, I can't have anything happen to you either."

"It won't. But you have to stay here. I'm going down there. You have to do as I ask. I can't risk you."

Her mouth went dry and her heart raced. "But I have to. This is my fight."

"I understand that," he gritted in frustration. "Lori, I can handle this. I can't handle if something happens to you."

Indecision rolled in a long wave through her. "I'll go with you but stay back. You can't ask me to do less than that. "

"Fine. Have it your way." He kissed her quickly again and then let her go.

But the tension between them was back, different from what it was before, but it was there. She knew he wanted to keep her safe but there was no way she wasn't going down there. They rolled their windows down and they could hear the low whine of the truck as it came across the pastures. It topped the hill and they could make out the outline of a truck and trailer.

They had come after their cattle. There was no doubt about it. They had scouted it last night and now they had come back to take what they wanted. *Or try,* Lori thought.

Trip got out of the truck. She slid over and followed him out the same door. He reached back inside and took his rifle from the gun rack on the back window. Lori wished she had brought hers—not that she'd ever used it for anything but target practice and shooting poisonous snakes. But she figured if she needed to protect herself or someone she loved she'd be able to take care of business… But no, she'd let him talk her out of it. "I wish I had my gun."

"You're not going to need your gun. I have mine but it's okay, you're going to stay back. Remember?"

"Right."

Frustrations of her own had her shifting from one boot to the other as they watched the trailer lights showing them exactly where the truck was going. They crept through the tall grass and she was thankful for her boots as she didn't relish the idea of stepping on any creepy snakes tonight. She might scream and that wouldn't be good.

They were half a football field length away when Trip stopped moving unexpectedly and she slammed into the back of him.

"Umph," she grunted then squeaked, "Sorry."

They waited as they could make out two men unloading horses. Of course, they'd brought horses. That was one thing about cattle rustling, rustlers had to know what they were doing when they stole cattle. They had to know how to cut what they wanted from the herd, and how to load them. It wasn't a skill set that everyone had. Which meant that a cattle rustler was normally a cowboy.

When the two mounted their horses, they rode toward the herd. Trip leaned back and whispered, "Let's go,"

He started across the pasture again, keeping low as

they took a parallel path down the hill and advanced toward the truck. Her adrenaline was high as she followed Trip.

And prayed that nothing went wrong.

Trip knew that Brice and Cooper were out there somewhere on the lookout for rustlers on their property. And so were Shane and Drake. Vance had stayed home after much persuasion so that he'd be fit to compete tomorrow night. He was in the running to make it to the finals again and he couldn't miss that opportunity.

There was a lot of ranch to watch over and he hoped they made it here before anything bad went down. He'd sent them a text but had no idea how far away they were.

Shane and Drake would stay home tomorrow night and keep watch on the ranch, looking for rustlers while everyone else tried to help at the rodeo.

They all understood that the rustlers had scouted the ranches and would be back quickly before the cattle were moved out of the pastures they'd been in when the rustlers had scoped them out.

He was worried about the stubborn, beautiful woman following him like a shadow. If he couldn't keep her safe… Even the thought of it had his stomach churning. He would keep her safe.

He leaned close to Lori. "I'm going in," he whispered. "You have your phone if something goes wrong I need you to stay here and make the call to 911 now that we know they're really intending to steal the cattle."

"Okay, but I'm not promising you that I'm going to stay here after I make the call. You take care of yourself."

"You better stay. You promised. Now make the call." He forced himself not to be distracted and then he made his way toward the rustlers. He thought there were four rustlers. Two on horses and two working the trailer.

He hoped these were the same people who'd taken the horses. If so, then maybe they'd get some answers. It was more important since he'd spilled his guts to Lori and now he needed more than ever for the stock to make it to the finals and let everyone know that the stock company was going to make it without the larger-than-life presence of Ray.

He needed to stand on his own if he was going to ask Lori to marry him. And he was going to ask her because he couldn't stand being apart from her any longer.

"Can we hurry this up," one of the men growled. "I got a bad feeling about this."

Trip reached the truck and hurried down the side of it and in between the tailgate and the cattle trailer. He peeked around the edge and this close could see the two men.

"I'm all for getting this over with. Tell Carter and Lomax to sort and load faster."

Carter and Lomax, two of the ranch hands he'd let go for making unsavory remarks about Lori when she took over for her dad. He'd fired them on the spot. And now the no-goods were stealing her cattle. Trip's blood boiled as he listened to them.

"Hurry up," the second rustler snapped. "You two act like you never sorted cattle before."

In answer, Carter and Lomax cut two heifers from the herd and made them charge the two cowboys working their mouths more than the gate to the trailer.

"Hey, watch out!" Simon growled. The third man's distinctive voice finally registered, and he remembered the cowboy's name. He didn't think he knew the fourth rustler. But he would.

Trip moved silently down the side of the trailer. The cattle they'd just run up into the trailer were making enough noise to drown out any noise he happened to make but Trip crouched low and moved quickly toward the man holding the trailer gate. He didn't stop until the barrel of his rifle was in Simon's back.

"What?"

"Nice and easy," Trip said. "And I won't have to hurt you. Now step out there. You too," he said to the other rustler.

"What do you think you're doing?" Simon asked, his voice hard.

"Getting you ready to go to jail. Now move. And call your buddies."

Suddenly, there was movement and the loud crack of a bullwhip sounded, instantly the cattle stampeded straight toward the trailer. The cowboys on horseback knew exactly what they were doing. Trip slammed tight against the side of the trailer while Simon was hit head-on by a cow he stumbled and went down and was trampled by the first cow. Trip yelled, "Yah." Waved his arms in hopes the cattle would see him in the darkness and he reached down and grasp Simon by the arm and drug him up and out of the way of the rest of the herd. The man was groaning and could barely stand. When the cattle had run past Trip looked around, and in the pale light he saw Lomax on horseback and he had a struggling, mad as a hornet Lori, laid over his saddle horn.

"Put me down," Lori yelled. She couldn't believe she'd let the rustler see her. But she'd been unable to stand it hiding in the weeds and had crept closer. And Ted Lomax had spotted her as she'd raced to get out of the path of the stampeding cattle. He'd ridden forward and yanked her up and across his horse like a sack of potatoes before she'd had a chance to scream.

"Hold still and I won't have to shoot your boyfriend."

"No! You wouldn't dare," she gasped. "You, you should know that I, I called the police and a whole posse is on the way." She thought of Trip calling the Presleys her posse. She knew they'd be out there somewhere. *Come on, Posse.*

"Put your rifle down, Trip," he demanded as if she hadn't spoken at all.

"Don't you dare put your rifle down, Trip," she yelled. "Lomax y'all are stealing cattle. That's not a hanging offense anymore! But killing us is—this is ridiculous. Take my stinking cattle. But don't do this."

"She's right," Trip said. "Don't make this any worse than it is. You can take the cattle. And you can even keep the five horses if you took them."

"I don't want to kill anyone," a man grunted.

Lori held her head up from where she dangled over the front shoulder of the horse. Simon, one of the men Trip had fired with Lomax. She bet Carter was out here too. "Good for you," she yelled.

"I was just in this to get back at them for firing us," he continued. "I don't want any part of killing."

"Me either," another man yelled.

Lori couldn't see him and didn't recognize him. She knew there was another man on horseback out here, she'd seen him when Lomax had grabbed her.

Now she saw him approaching. But in the dark, she couldn't see his face with his hat pulled low. But she'd bet that was Carter.

"Carter take the rifle from Trip."

Suddenly, she saw the rider level his shotgun but instead of pointing it at Trip he shoved it into the unsuspecting Lomax's ribs.

"No can do—"

Lori gasped—*Cooper Presley* was sitting in the saddle.

"What?" Lomax growled.

"No what's, ands or ifs," Cooper drawled. "I'm a crack shot and a hothead. And you happen to have one of my very favorite females in all the world dumped over your horse in a very uncomfortable position. So, I'd think long and hard about what this shotgun can do at close range. And I'd toss that pistol you're holding over there to the side." She heard the sound of hooves and out of the darkness five more horses and riders moved in and flanked Lomax. They all leveled a firearm at the man sharing a horse with her.

Lomax said something vulgar then tossed the pistol to the ground.

Instantly, Trip came to her and helped her scramble off the saddle horn. He pulled her into his arms and held her.

"Are you okay?" he asked.

"I'm better now," she managed and wrapped her arms around his neck as he carried her away from Lomax and his horse.

"Thank you all for showing up," she said later, as the police got there and took the four rustlers away and she looked around the group of cowboys. Trip had his arm around her shoulders holding her close.

"Yeah, thank all of you. And Cooper, that was a pretty good trick you did on the horse."

His brothers all chuckled, the tension was gone, and they were all relaxing a bit.

"You should have seen him," Vance said. We had just reached the area when the cattle stampeded and he jumped out of the truck and streaked across the pasture and grabbed that rider off his horse before he knew what hit him. I had followed him and he handed him off to me then swung up into the saddle and rode the horse back toward y'all like he was one of them."

The night was lit up with truck lights and so Cooper's cocky grin was visible. "Hey, I figured it was our best shot of getting close."

"And you were right," Marcus said. "So, they said they didn't know anything about the stolen horses. And they took our cattle just to throw everyone off so no one would suspect them."

"Yes, that's what they said," Trip said. "So, as unbelievable as it is, we had cattle rustlers and horse thieves at the same time."

"That is beating the odds on bad luck," Drake said, shaking his head. "Any more news from the Knights?"

"I'll call them in the morning and tell them what happened and I'll see if there is any more news. They'll all be at the Stockyards. Speaking of that, I guess we better all call it a night. Lori, let's get you home."

"Okay, I'm too wound up to sleep, but maybe I can. Thanks again, fellas. I'm a lucky woman to have all of you."

And she was. When they reached the ranch, Trip walked her to her door and held her. "I don't want to let you go," he said against her temple.

"I know. I love you. I was so scared when they were threatening to shoot you."

"And I was terrified when I saw they had you. I don't want to ever lose you, Lori."

"I love hearing you say that. You won't."

And she went to bed that night with that thought on her mind.

CHAPTER ELEVEN

As planned, they drove the horses to the Fort Worth Stockyards, checked them in and then met with the Knights in the lobby of the historic Stockyard Hotel. Lori loved the old hotel, she'd spent many nights in this hotel when she and her dad came to the Stockyards. She loved the history of the place and the beautiful furnishings. She loved the way the old stairs creaked when she walked up them, and she love the slow-moving elevator.

It was the perfect place to meet, because since her dad had loved it too, so it felt as if he was sitting in on the meeting.

Only two of the Knight brothers had come, Jesse, the ex-military policeman and then Sean the veterinarian who took care of the rodeo stock while at the events. After they all greeted each other they got down to business.

Jesse's smile turned serious. "I think we have a good lead. Michael flew to Oklahoma City to check it out and will hopefully have answers before the rodeo is over."

"That's where Kramer's outfit's at," Trip said.

"Yes," Sean agreed. "It is. He's going to do some undercover poking around."

"I hope he's careful. I want our horses back but not at the expense of someone getting hurt." A thankfulness swept over Lori as she stood there. Her daddy might not be here but she was surrounded by a tremendous amount of amazing men, counting these three men, the five Presley brothers, and their dad, and then Trip too. She wasn't sure what she'd done to deserve them but she was thankful. She had the best team a woman could ask for on her side. She felt as if her daddy had been unable to stand by her side so he sent the best he could round up. Lori's heart felt like it would burst. And yet, she also wanted to stand on her own feet and be a part of the solution.

"Michael can take care of himself, so don't worry," Jesse assured her. "We have a man digging around at Kramer's ranch. He's searching the place for any signs of your horses and has a suspicion he might know where they are. We decided one of us needed to be there. He'll be in touch. In the meantime, we're going to hang out here and personally keep our eyes open. This is the WRC and we want this resolved as quickly as possible."

"So, do I," she said, glancing at Trip.

"We all want that," Sean said. "Trip tells me that Vance Presley and his brothers are here looking out for your interests too. If we all have our ears open to the conversations and actions around us something, even something small might come to light."

"I hope so," she said, just as Sean's phone rang.

"We all do," he said as he unclipped his phone from its clip on his belt. "Excuse me." He moved away from them all as he answered the call.

It didn't last long before he ended it. "I need to head out. There's a lame bull that needs my attention."

"That's fine," Jesse said, then frowned. "Let us know how that turns out. I need to check with the secretary but I believe Kramer has stock that could benefit from this."

"I don't like the sound of this." Trip frowned.

"I'll let you know what I find out after I look at the animal." Sean slipped out the door not wasting any more time talking.

Lori was restless. "I think I'll go check on my horses. I'm glad everyone is here, Daddy would be very appreciative of all the help. I know this may not be all targeted at the Calhoun Ranch and mine and Trip's stock company but either way it needs to stop. Hopefully, Sean will find that the bull he's looking at is lame for no some simple problem. But anyway, call me if any info turns up. And I'll do the same. I'll see y'all later at the rodeo."

"I'll come with you," Trip said goodbye to Jesse and headed out with her.

They left the hotel and walked toward the arena. There were a small group of western clad singers entertaining people on the steps of the Stock Exchange and the lively music and hustle of tourists made the street a lively place. When she heard the sound of cattle mooing she stared down the street and saw the daily cattle drive coming their way. The reenactment was put on daily for all the tourists at the Stockyards. Lori watched Longhorns and cowboys pass by and again thought of her dad.

She looked at Trip. "I used to love coming here as a girl. I remember the first time I saw them run cattle through here. Daddy picked me up and put me on his shoulders to watch the Longhorns and the cowboys." Those memories seemed etched in her mind more than normal this weekend. It had been a while since she'd come to Fort Worth and the Stockyards. So much history was etched in this place and she and her father's memories were forever etched there for her as deeply as Texas history and the cattle drives of the early days were etched in the history.

"I have memories too with my dad. We loved the Stockyard Museum and eating at the Cattleman's Steakhouse…that was a treat for a little kid."

"Yes, it was, I'm sure." She shot him an understanding smile. "I hope we have a new memory here that includes finding our horses."

"That would be a fantastic memory for us. I'm just in shock that someone would risk everything to do something like this."

"Me too. But when someone gets themselves into financial trouble like he's obviously in there is no telling what they'll do."

They entered the Coliseum and headed to the stalls. Cooper spotted them and came over. "Hey, glad you're here. There was a guy hanging around earlier. I watched him and he just seemed overly interested in your stock. I finally asked him if he needed any help with anything and he didn't waste any time disappearing. Also, heard through the grapevine that a bull is lame and the owner is furious."

Trip was studying their horses. "Sean Knight is on his way to look at the bull. This guy you saw, what does your gut tell you? Did you think he was up to no good?"

"I did, I kept watching at first to see if he was going to make a move but no deal. He finally just irritated me and I wanted to see if he'd spook."

"And he did," she said.

"Oh, yes he did. The question is why? Like the Knights have stated this Kramer has reason for wanting your horses out of the show. But it seems too easy."

"That's what I'm thinking, but then, desperation leads to sloppiness," Trip said. "I think Kramer is a real jerk, but stupid? It's hard for me to believe and yet it's not looking good for him."

"I'll stick around back here during the rodeo as they take the horses into the chutes."

"Thanks," Lori said, as she moved to the fence to study her horses. They all acted like they were in good spirits and that usually meant they were going to put on a good show, which was exactly what she needed from them. With her top five out, these fellas needed to step up and give the bucking performances of their lives.

A few hours later the rodeo was in full swing Trip

couldn't chase the feeling away that something wasn't right. Maybe he was feeling overly suspicious but his gut was telling him something was wrong or going to be wrong.

They had men spread out all over the place. Jesse had gone behind the chutes to hang out with the bull riders and they knew that Sean would be around back there too. Since the bull that had been lame had been taken out and one of Kramer's backup bulls had taken its place.

When it was finally time for the saddle bronc competition Trip could tell Lori was nervous. He reached out and took her hands. "Relax. It's going to be okay. Nothing is going to happen to our horses. We have too many eyes on the ground watching and listening. And Cooper is not going to let anything happen back there. He'll call if we're needed."

"But we need them to figure this out. Not just make it through. When this rodeo ends and we don't have our horses, then we don't make the finals."

He wanted and needed the horses to make the finals, he had something to prove but seeing the worry on her face, he realized there were more important things than proving he had what it took to keep a business successful.

He pulled her into his arms. "I want to find the horses. I want them safe and you know I want to compete and show this company is strong. But if we don't meet the deadline, that's just the way it's going to be. We keep going." He kissed her gently with a brief brush of his lips to hers. She stared up at him as if stunned.

"But, what about us?"

He loved the feel of her in his arms. "We're fine. We'll get our situation figured out when everything is settled. But right now, try not to worry. I just want you to realize life doesn't end if we don't have horses in the finals."

She took a deep breath. "Okay, I'll try to relax. Dad would have said something similar."

"Yes, I believe he would have. Your daddy was a very smart, wise man." He kissed her forehead.

She turned deeply serious. "Yes, he was, he hired you." She placed her arms around his waist and hugged him.

Satisfaction coursed through Trip. "Thank you, that means a lot to me."

"I'm glad we've made it to this point," she said, and the worry in her expression eased. "I'm glad to have you at my side."

"*Up next Vance Presley*," the announcer called over the loudspeaker. "Riding Dream Wrecker."

They both faced the arena and watched as Vance lowered himself into the chute and settled on the back of the bronc. He hadn't drawn one of theirs but instead, had drawn of all horses one of Kramer's. The horse was restless and jumped in the chute causing Vance to scramble back up on the chute bars with his boots braced on either side of the rowdy saddle bronc. The cowboys holding the bucking horses' reins put pressure on, trying to settle Dream Wrecker down and after a couple of seconds, Vance yanked on his hat then lowered himself back down.

Trip could see Jesse's head over the stall rungs where he had moved in close and was studying the horse. There was nothing unusual about a restless saddle bronc though. They were high strung and ready to rock-n-roll in an event.

In the next moment, the gate opened, and the horse blasted from the chute, bucking and spinning trying with everything it had to toss Vance to the dirt. Vance rode with all the show and skill of the best, arms back, knees working as he moved with the rhythm of the saddle bronc. One thing about the cowboy, he was one of the best and his trips to the finals were a testament to that. Tonight was no different as he rode Dream Wrecker to the buzzer. The horse was bucking like mad as the pickup men rode in hard to help Vance get off the back of the horse safely. It was always a dangerous moment when the cowboy tried to jump from the bucking horse. The two pickup men came alongside the horse and one reached for the bucking cinch while the other tried to move in so Vance could grab his shoulders and swing off Dream Weaver and jump to the ground with the protection of the pickup horse between him and the bronc.

It was not easy when the horse was freaking out as it seemed this one was doing. Finally, Vance managed to throw himself off the horse while holding onto one of the pickup men's shoulders then slide to the ground unharmed. The good-looking cowboy grinned as his boots hit the dirt. He yanked his hat off his head and fanned it to the roaring crowd as he jogged to the fence.

"Whew," Lori gasped. "Always a showman. I was worried."

"Yeah, that horse was hyped up good."

"Well, they're trying hard for rough stock that will give the guys a tough ride. The tougher the ride the farther the horse goes."

"True, ours are great in the arena but that just seemed off to me. Let's go down there. I want to talk to Vance and Jesse."

She heard the skepticism in his voice and when he started down the bleachers she followed.

CHAPTER TWELVE

They reached the bottom of the stands and headed toward the stock area. Trip wanted to hear what Vance had to say about that horse. And he wanted to hear what Jesse thought too. There had been some drugging of stock a while back and he couldn't help wondering if that had happened again. Kramer was obviously in over his head and desperate. But he didn't want to say anything more to Lori until his suspicions were confirmed. Sean could find out with a simple blood test if the others were suspicious too.

Or maybe he was just being overly touchy where anything that had to do with Kramer was concerned. By most people's standards that had been an amazing competitor in that ring. Not a drugged-up horse that could hurt himself or his rider.

Speak of the devil, Kramer moved from a group of men and slid in front of them blocking their path. He was a short man with a thick waist and he liked to wear his shirt unbuttoned two buttons too many to expose the gold chain he wore around his neck. But his biggest and worse accessory was his shadow, the six feet four-inch cowboy that Trip and many of the others referred to as his *goon*. The man crossed his tree-trunk sized arms and leveled a glare at them.

"Kramer," Trip acknowledged him. He stepped closer to Lori when he heard her intake of air when she realized who the man was. Trip had forgotten that she still hadn't met the man who it was looking more and more like stole their horses.

"Jensen. Miss Calhoun," Kramer drawled in what sounded more like a snarl. "I've been wondering when I was going to run into you. What do you think you're up to?"

Lori shot Trip a questioning look, but he kept his expression stone cold as he returned his gaze to Kramer. It took everything he had to hold his temper in check. "We've been right here. The question is what have you been up to?"

The man blustered. "What does that mean?"

"You asked the question first. We're trying to run a stock business. Trying to figure out who took our horses. You wouldn't happen to know anything about all that, would you?"

He turned red-faced. "Are you accusing me of something?"

Trip cocked his head to the side and stared hard at the bodyguard when he took a step forward. "I'd back up, hoss," he demanded. "We're just having a conversation here that we did not initiate. Kramer either answers my question or steps aside. We're trying to congratulate our good friend on a great ride. Looks like Vance got the better of your bronc."

"I don't believe I've had the pleasure of an introduction, but I'm assuming you are Mr. Kramer and the owner of Vance's ride moments ago?" Lori didn't look at all intimidated.

"That's me," he huffed. "My horse almost got him off. It was still a tough ride and a high score. Presley got lucky."

"You think? I beg to differ." Trip goaded him on purpose. Hoping to see what the man would do. If he had taken their horses then he wanted to push the man and see what happened. All he could hope was that Michael was having good luck on the ground at the man's ranch right now.

"My horses are better than the Calhoun Stock. Your outfit is the one that's had the lucky breaks in the lineup, getting the lesser riders and making your horses look better while mine draw the tougher contenders and it makes them look like a lesser ride. You know it's true." He glared at Lori. "Your daddy always had the luck on his side."

Lori stiffened. "My daddy worked hard and believed in making his own luck happen through his hard work."

Kramer's eyes narrowed. "You're a smart a—"

Trip cut him off, "Watch your mouth, Kramer. Don't

start insulting my partner."

The man cut angry eyes at him. "From what I hear she's your boss. You're just her lackey."

Trip let the cutting words slide off of him, knowing Kramer was just baiting him. "I think we're done here. We have a rider to congratulate. Step aside."

"For now." Kramer moved away and *his* lackey moved with him.

Trip took Lori's arm and moved her past them. He could feel the fight in her in the stiffness of her arm and could see it in her eyes and the square of her shoulders and jaw. She was brewing for a fight. He tugged harder when she hesitated and glared at Kramer.

"He's my partner. The best there is." Trip pulled hard and forced her to move past Kramer.

"Well isn't that just so sweet. She's taking up for you," Kramer snarled sarcastically.

Trip clamped his mouth shut.

"How dare you say something like that," Lori blurted out. "Who do you think you are, you little twerp—"

Trip grabbed Lori by the arm and hauled her into the crowd and toward the rough stock chutes.

"Why are you pulling on me? I had something to say," she demanded, yanking to get loose from him but he held on tight.

"Because we'd said enough, and he's not worth wasting any more breath on."

"But what he said isn't true."

"I know that. I'm fine. I crossed that line a while back. Okay? But you didn't need to go pushing any more buttons on the dude than you already had."

"Fine," she snapped. "But he had it coming."

Yeah, that was true. Trip let the words play in his head but said nothing as he tried to ignore the pricks to his pride. Tried to not let the jabs Kramer was trying to hit him with dig in, but deny as he might, deep down the words struck their mark.

Everything about the run-in with Kramer made Lori's skin crawl. He had intentionally insulted Trip and her dad and tried to go after her but Trip had stopped him. She wished she'd been able to stop him from insulting Trip. The same ole story always seemed to jump between them. She knew once again she'd had bait tossed at her but Trip had managed to keep her from taking it too far. She had to get better at holding her tongue. But, well shoot, the man was a sleazeball.

Vance, Jesse, and Seth were in deep conversation with Marcus Presley when they walked up.

"What's going on?" she asked.

"Something wrong with that ride?" Trip studied them with penetrating eyes that Lori felt all the way to her toes.

"We have our suspicions," Jesse said. "We're not sure if the horse was hyped up to ride harder or what but Vance did a great job."

Sean did not look happy. "I'm going to test it and see, might disqualify Vance's ride but, again, substance abuse is easy to detect so if he drugged Dream Wrecker then he's desperate."

"The deal is," Vance said. "He didn't ride much different from a regular tough ride. If he's drugged, then it wasn't enough to draw attention to anyone but us. And that's because we're looking for anything that might point a finger at Kramer."

"True," Marcus said. "We could be overly observant. Lori, is something wrong, honey? You looked angry when you walked up here."

"Yes. I just had the unpleasant opportunity to meet Kurt Kramer. The man is awful."

Grunts of agreement made the rounds from everyone around her.

"You stay away from him," Trip said. "I got the distinct feeling that this isn't just about rodeo status but is personal. Your daddy never said a lot about Kramer. He just didn't like him or trust him after that incident with our horse. But when it happened, he also didn't seem surprised. I'm wondering if there is history there we don't know about. Marcus do you know anything?"

Marcus looked thoughtful, as if searching his memory. If anyone knew anything it would be Marcus since he and her dad had been best friends since their early years.

"Well, I know your dad always said Kurt, or Kramer, as everyone seems to call him nowadays, held grudges for way too long. Said it wasn't healthy."

"But why would he say that?" she asked.

"Yeah," Trip spoke up. "He never said that to me. He just told me to keep a close watch on everything after we suspected him of hurting our horse."

"For one, he used to compete with us in the rodeo and he wasn't as good as us. But it seemed he could never best your dad. I think there was a woman he had a thing for too that wouldn't give him the time of day because she was too busy chasing after your dad. But your dad didn't reciprocate the infatuation and she still wouldn't have anything to do with Kramer. Maybe that's what Ray meant. When it came to talking about women Ray didn't say much and I didn't either."

"He didn't tolerate any disrespect toward women," Trip said. "I know that for certain. So I can see why he'd keep his mouth closed even when he was being chased by one he didn't want to pursue. So if Kramer has sour apples about that, then the man is putting the blame where it doesn't belong."

"That's for certain," Marcus agreed.

Lori took a deep breath trying to digest everything. "So do you think all this could be from an old grudge about being rejected by a woman?"

Every man in the group looked at her and shrugged.

"Men have died for lesser reasons all through history," Jesse said. "Right now, that's all we've got, that and his financial problems. He's looking for someone to blame."

She couldn't believe it could be that simple. It was ridiculous. But it was true that people did crazy things.

"Let's call a meeting with everyone over at the stock pens," Trip said. "I'm sure Cooper and Brice are wondering what's going on.

"That'd be great," Drake said, looking as unhappy as

she was. "When are the cops going to get involved with this?"

"We're waiting to see what Michael and the local sheriff's department he's working with in Oklahoma can come up with."

"I see," Drake said.

Jesse and Sean led the way out of the crowded chute area and she and Trip followed.

"Are you okay?" he asked.

"I'm mad," she said. "And confused. It just doesn't make sense." She heard someone call her name and turned to see Kelly, a former rodeo friend from college. Her spirits lifted for a moment. "Hey, go on without me. I'll be there as soon as I say hi to an old friend."

He didn't look happy. "I'll stay with you. I don't want you hanging out alone—"

"I'm fine, Trip. I'll be right there. Truth is I need a break from all this and visiting with Kelly for a moment sounds perfect."

He didn't look happy as Kelly got closer through the throng of people. "Fine. But if you're not back in fifteen minutes, I'll come looking."

She frowned. "Stop worrying. I'll be there when I get through but it won't be long. I'm not going to keep everyone waiting."

"Okay, but call if you need me."

She laughed and shook her head. "Go. I'm fine." As soon as he headed off, she turned and met Kelly in a big hug. Talking to an old friend would help. She was fed up with the craziness going on around her.

CHAPTER THIRTEEN

Trip caught up with Jesse and the Presleys after leaving Lori to visit with her friend. He felt uncomfortable leaving her and was on edge with the way the conversation had gone with Kramer. Something had happened between Kramer and Ray Calhoun. And it was reasonable that someone could hold a grudge for this long. People, as Jess had said, did terrible things for a lot less this than being jealous over a woman and being rejected.

Not only had Kramer had a woman reject him because she was crazy about Ray, it was a woman that Ray hadn't wanted. That would be unsettling for a guy like Kramer. And then Kramer had gone into the rough stock business and so had Ray. And Ray was more successful.

Yeah, Trip got it. He could see where that would grate at a guy. Especially a guy who wasn't dealing with a full deck it seemed.

But the fact that he hadn't made his whole move until now, after Ray was gone, fit. He was fairly certain that Kramer had poisoned that horse that time and, he was sure Ray figured it out. For all Trip knew, since Ray hadn't told a story on that, Ray may have had a meeting of the mind with Kramer about that incident that Trip was not privy to. He could only imagine what a man like Ray said to a man like Kramer. As intimidating as Ray was, with his larger-than-life personality, and being so well liked, versus the little twerp that Kramer was, Trip could see where Kramer would've probably been shaking in his boots. Until Ray died and his daughter took over. And his financial problems became so terrible and he became desperate. He figured he could pick on Trip and Lori. He could take their business to ruin and then he would get jobs. When Trip reached the others, and they met up with Cooper and Brice, he relayed what he thought. They all looked unfazed by his assessment.

Marcus was the first to speak up. "I agree with you, I can see where Ray would've probably gone to him, he wouldn't have tiptoed around the situation. If he thought Kramer had hurt his animal Ray would have confronted him. He might not have told you or me because that's the kind of man Ray was. But I guarantee you that behind closed doors, man to man—Ray handled it.

And that's why his animals didn't get messed with again. But now, like you say, he's desperate, and he's just the kind of man who would pick on a woman—not that you're a woman but you know what I mean. Ray was

Lori's daddy, and he's gone and Lori is here. Lori own's the ranch. It's more about her. To be frank."

Trip understood it. He knew Marcus didn't mean any harm by what he said, it was the truth. No matter how hard he worked, no matter how much the success of the rough stock business would and could ultimately be because of his promotion and work, in the end, it would always be that Ray Calhoun's daughter owned the ranch and the business that Ray began. And Trip had just bought into it.

He loved Lori. But could he live with that? The truth of their situation was staring him in the face. But right now, it didn't matter. Right now, it was about getting this business with Kramer settled, getting their horses back and moving forward.

Jesse's phone rang. He pulled it from its holster. "It's Michael." He stepped away from everybody and they all watched as he listened. His expression was intense. Then furious. The call didn't last long and he hung up and stalked to them, his expression grave.

"They found the horses. Michael was relentless and his informant worked hard to help him. It was time to go looking while Kramer and his goons weren't around. It took a little while but they found them on some property Kramer leases way in the backcountry in a barn. They've been neglected all this time. No feed. They're not in good shape but are being looked after now."

Trip spun on his boot heel, fury swept through him. He was going for Kramer.

Marcus and Cooper stepped in front of him

"Hold on," Cooper said.

"Yeah, son," Marcus agreed. "You're in no shape to go after Kramer. Take a deep breath."

"You'd rip his head off." Drake and Brice stepped up to help block him.

"The police are on their way," Jesse told him. "They are probably on the premises as we speak. We need to tell Lori."

The rodeo was ending and people were moving out of the stands. It was a rough time to be trying to find her. Trip suddenly got his senses back. "Yeah, we need to find her. I don't want Kramer getting near her. If he's already been tipped off. Then who knows what he'll do if he feels cornered."

Lori was making her way through the rough stock pens when she spotted a group of police officers enter the building at the end of the corridor. One of them stood out in his cowboy hat, starched white shirt with the shining star pinned over his heart, even at a distance she was pretty sure he was a U.S. Marshal. Her gut told her once more something wasn't right.

She was, of all places, near Kramer's stock pens when she spotted them. And they were coming this way. People were parting the way for them as they came down the corridor. She looked around just as she was grabbed around her neck and she was yanked hard against a soft body.

"They're not going to pin this on me," the distinctive voice of Kramer growled in her ear.

She yanked harder. "Let me go," she demanded.

"Hold still," he growled.

She was uncertain of what had happened but obviously, something had. "Let me go," she gasped as he tightened his arm around her neck. For a small man, he had surprising strength in his short arms. She tried to kick him in the knee and then grunted. "They're going to stop you."

"Kramer," Trip yelled from the distance. "Let her go, it's over. The police are here. We know what you did our horses."

"This is the police. Let her go and put your hands up."

Lori heard the anger in Trip's voice and suddenly she wasn't just mad, she was worried. She brought her hands up to grasp the arm wrapped around her neck. She was a little taller than Kramer and he had her yanked hard against him, forcing her to lean back. It was awkward and made his grip on her throat that much more painful. She coughed which only caused him to hold tighter as he started backing them up. "Where," she gasped. "are you going? Give up. You're done." She coughed again, her gaze finding Trip in the now cleared out corridor. People had scrambled out of there as fast as they could get to safety. Trip stood out in the wide-open glaring Kramer down. She couldn't find the lawmen in her vision but they were to the left while Trip and the Presleys and the Knights were to the right. She could see them, her posse standing behind Trip.

She felt the hard bite of a pistol dig into her back.

"I've got a pistol and I'll use it on your girlfriend."

"Don't make this worse on yourself," the lawman called. Let the lady go and you won't get hurt."

"I'm walking out of here with her," he yelled, loosening his grip on her momentarily.

Lori sucked in a breath. "Why are you doing this?"

"Your daddy ruined me. If it hadn't been for him always getting the luck—"

Lori was dealing with a madman. He had lost all reasoning where her daddy was concerned and blamed everything wrong in his life of her dad.

"Your bad judgment is what cost you, Kramer. And you're making more bad choices right now. Let Lori go. Do the right thing." Trip was moving cautiously toward them. On the other side, the law had pulled their weapons. Lori suddenly realized someone might not come out of this alive.

Her knees were weak. "Trip, stop," she called. Fear for him was overwhelming. "Get out of the way."

As if in answer Kramer pulled his pistol from her ribs and pointed it at Trip.

Trip's heart hammered as he watched the woman he loved

being choked and held captive by Kramer. He stared at the gun pointing at him and looked past the madman to see the lawmen fanning out. One was over inside the stock pen and moving toward Kramer using cattle as his shield.

"I'm walking out of here so move out of the way. All of you. Get in that crosswalk and let me pass or I'll shoot her."

"Don't do that," the U.S. Marshal warned. "Put your weapon down, there's no way out of this."

"Kramer stop this while you can," Lori urged, feeling the man's desperation and feeling her own as she watched Trip hover between holding back or charging her captor. Fear for him held her in its icy grip. She couldn't bear to lose him. Their eyes locked and panic seized her as she saw his gaze flinch, saw him step forward. "No," she shouted, struggling to stop him from stepping toward the gun leveled at him.

As if in slow motion she saw him move, felt Kramer panic, his arm jerked and on instinct she stomped hard on his boot while elbowing him in the gut and twisting hard—as the sound of the gun fired…

In that same instant, Kramer's arm loosened, and she was free, she stumbled to the ground as two more shots were fired and Kramer fell in the dirt beside her. Her gaze was locked on Trip.

He dropped to his knees as a bloodstain spread across his shoulder and then he fell face first in the dirt.

CHAPTER FOURTEEN

"Don't you dare leave me, Trip Jensen…"

Trip struggled to roll over, his shoulder hurt like he'd been kicked by a rampaging, two-thousand-pound bucking bull but all he was focused on was Lori's sweet voice. She was okay.

"I'm not going anywhere," he managed as she helped him onto his back. "I'm staying right here with you, darlin'" He drawled, trying hard not to slur his words, fighting to stay conscious. "You're a beautiful sight."

"Oh, Trip, I thought…" she cried. "I thought I'd lost you."

"Let me in here," Sean Knight said, pushing through the throng of friends hovering over Trip and Lori.

Trip winced when Sean immediately applied hard pressure to his wound.

"It's your shoulder. You'll have a scar but you'll live. Thanks to Lori fighting like a wildcat to knock that fools aim off."

Trip gave her a grin. "Seems I owe you my life," he said, wiping the tears from her face with his free hand.

"And I owe you mine," she said through her tears. Heard a smile try to sound in her words. "You shouldn't have done that."

"Done what? Try to save the woman I love?"

She laughed and her smile sent joy raging through him. "I love you too. But still, thank God and the Marshal's good aim we're going to live to enjoy that love."

He felt his head spinning. "Exactly what I was aiming for," he said and then everything went black.

Two days later

"Okay, open that trailer," Lori instructed. Michael Knight had warned her that the horses had lost weight but were doing good. Sean had driven to Oklahoma straight from the rodeo after the ambulance had gotten there for Trip. He'd wanted to check them out and monitor their wellbeing and transport back to the ranch. He and Michael had gone out of their way to take care of them. Jesse Knight had remained in Fort Worth helping handle any legal issues as all that Kurt Kramer had done came to light. She would always be grateful to the Knight Investigation Agency for what they'd done.

But as she glanced around the group waiting with her and Trip, her heart was full. The handsome Presleys were all gathered around the round pen, including Carson Anderson, their cousin. He strode toward her and hugged her.

"Lori, I'm so sorry this was going on and I couldn't help." He stepped back and grabbed Trip's hand. "I'm glad you're okay."

"Me too," Trip grinned. "And we knew you had your hands full."

Lori felt bad for Carson, and the ongoing struggle he had with his little girl's mother. "You've got your own priorities. Is Julie okay?"

Carson looked troubled but faked a smile. "She's fine, just at that age that she really needs a mom. And her mom…well, she's a little too busy to care."

"She's the loser in all of this. Julie has you and she's a lucky little girl." His wife had run off and left him with a baby to raise and he'd done a good job but Lori knew he worried that he wasn't good enough and that his little girl missed not having a mother around. He, like all his cousins was a good, good man and she hoped one day he'd take a chance on love once more.

"If you need anything while Trip is recovering please call me. I'll be home now."

"Thanks, Marcus has assured me that if there is anything I need while Trip is recovering all I need to do is ask and they'll take care of it. So, you all are amazing I'm sure I'll have all the help I can handle."

"Thanks for the offer," Trip said. "I appreciate the backup."

"I'm here if you need me. You might need to sit down, you look a bit pale still."

"Heading that way with him now." Lori said as Carson headed back to the fence.

She looked at Trip. No one had estimated Trip's determination to be here today. His shoulder had needed extensive surgery, and he'd lost a lot of blood but he'd gotten his release papers this morning and was standing beside her. His good arm was draped over her shoulders and Lori felt love and security within his shadow. God had been good, and he was still here with her.

Kramer wasn't. He'd died instantly when he'd fired that second shot the U. S. Marshal had fired at him and his bullet hadn't missed. Lori still couldn't believe that he'd blamed all of his bad choices and subsequent bad luck on her daddy. And that he'd felt it was his right to try to ruin what Ray Calhoun had worked so hard to build.

But that was all behind them. Her horses would be ready for the finals. They'd been given a reprieve from the next rodeo and Sean had said they'd be ready for the next rodeo on the circuit and qualify to participate in the big show, the National Finals in Vegas.

Harvey sat on a horse in the arena waiting on the rough stock horses to be released. He had come to her immediately when she arrived home and apologized for acting so negative since losing the horses and said he'd been defensive when he should have been helpful. He'd also asked if he could help care for the horses so they could be ready for the finals. She'd agreed and felt relief that they could start over since her daddy had liked Harvey and valued his contribution to the ranch.

"Here they come," Trip said, close to her ear. "Don't be too upset. Remember Sean said they're doing good."

She nodded as Michael pulled the trailer gate open and the horses ran out of the trailer and into the holding pen. She gasped. "Oh, how could anyone do that to horses?" Her horses were thin from just two weeks without feed, not as bad as some of the wild Mustangs the Presleys and their rescue program took in. But still, they were in a state of neglect. "Thankfully we got to them," she said. "If Kramer wasn't already dead I'd probably be heading to the jailhouse to give him a piece of my mind. How could he?"

"He was a messed-up man sometimes nothing explains it."

"Yeah. I guess so." She turned to him. "I'm so glad you're home. You need to sit down."

He smiled and hugged her to him. "I'm fine. We need to talk," he said and then led her away from the arena.

"Hey," Cooper called from where he and Vance were standing with their arms on the arena rungs studying the horses. "Where are you two lovebirds heading?"

Trip chuckled. "None of your business Presley, this is between me and my lady."

"Oh, your lady," his friend teased. "Well, y'all go on then and I hope you come back in a few minutes and give us some good news."

"Yeah," Vance added with a wink. "Good news. I think it's time for us to have a party around here. If you know what I mean."

Trip laughed and Lori shook her head and chuckled. "I kind of like the idea of a party too," she said and then hugging him tight they walked into the barn.

Trip stopped outside his office and turned to pull her close with his good arm. "I love you, Lori. And I've struggled with objection after objection as to why I can't ask you to be my wife. I don't have what you have and I might not ever have enough to equal what you have. That rankles on a man, but, your ranch aside, I can build something with you with the rough stock business that we can share together. I like that. But most of all I like the idea of building a life with you. I'm tired of putting it off. Of not telling you how much I love you. It's eating away at me and the other night when Kramer had you all I could think about was all the time we'd wasted. I don't want to spend another hour without you in my life. I can take anything but that. Will you marry me?"

Her arms were already around his waist but they tightened and her eyes were bright with tears. "I have waited so long to hear you say that. Yes, yes and yes. I love you and want to start our lives together. Now, as soon as possible." She carefully leaned into him and he kissed her as the sunbeam from the entrance of the barn spotlighted them and the warmth of her love spread through him.

"Then I do believe we're ready for that party."

She touched his face with tender fingers. "Trip, I've waited my whole life for this party. It's going to be amazing."

"You're amazing," he said, and then he settled his lips on hers and kissed her with all the love in his heart…

It was a long time before they left the barn to share their news.

CHAPTER ONE

"You need a wife."

"Those are fighting words." Carson Andrews shot his cousin a scowl. "Had the one and never another and you know it. Why would you even say that?"

"For one thing, it's been two years, Carson. It may be time to move on." Cooper Presley hitched a brow and shoved a newspaper at Carson. "But if that's not cool then you need a wife for a day-just a day that's all I'm saying. Read that ad and you'll understand."

Baffled, Carson stared down at the newspaper.

Single males in need of a bride for a day? This is

strictly an at-your-service business proposition. Absolutely no romance involved. Do you need the eyes of a woman to help plan and/or set up an event or decorate a space with your personal interest and taste in mind, but with an added touch of your bride—if you had one? Then call Bride for Hire and let me do the work...

"That right there is a bona fide perfect solution for your situation." Cooper grinned at him. "A little unconventional but still, you need a woman's touch. And she's just in Fort Worth, so that's not so far away that she couldn't come out here to help you out. It's worth a call at least."

Carson looked around the kitchen. It was about as featureless as a hospital room: Nothing on the walls. The counter held a coffee pot and a can of coffee beside it. And the living room beyond the bar area was just as plain. He thought of April's room and frowned. It wasn't much better with the only decorations being a floor full of scattered toys and a bed—at least it did have a colorful comforter.

A knot formed in Carson's gut. "You're right. As much as I hate to admit it, I could use someone to help get this place into shape. With April turning five at the end of the month, I guess I need to start learning how to decorate and bake cookies and give her what she is missing."

Cooper laughed. "They do make those kind you buy at the grocery store and just cut up then bake. I don't think the situation is so bad you have to break out the flour and start burning down the house."

"Hey, I could do it if I set my mind to it. And who says you could do any better? Last I counted, you and your four brothers were all still single and cared more about your horses than decorating."

Cooper squinted in the sunshine. "That'd be an accurate account for certain but we don't have a little girl who needs to be wearing tutus and having tea parties and such."

Carson shot his cousin an exasperated glare. "I've been having tea parties for over two years now, so don't even go there."

"Well, that's just great but you're falling down in other areas."

His mind churning, Carson led the way across the wide expanse of yard to the barn. There was a round pen off the back where a huge black bull waited. Carson was putting him in the sale in two weeks at Cooper's family ranch in Ransom Creek and Cooper was here to see him.

Cooper stopped at the fence and squinted at Carson. "Why haven't you asked one of the women around here in Bride to help you out?"

"Not a good idea. I'm not interested in starting anything up with anyone from Bride. I know there are a few ladies in town who'd welcome the thought of coming out here and helping me, they have made that clear, and they're nice ladies, for the most part-there are a few I avoid at all cost. I don't want to mislead anyone into thinking I'm going to need a woman hanging around for a future with me. There is no future with me. I've been through the wedding fiasco and it won't happen again."

Cooper looked skeptical. "It's not like you got jilted like that bride this town put that statue up for. Choosing one bad bride is no reason not to start thinking it would happen again."

"I'm not getting married again, Coop. Ever. I'm going to raise April, put up with her mother when she shows up for visits—if she shows up, and that's all I'm ready for at this point."

"But it's been two years. You aren't even dating again, are you?"

"Nope. I am not," Carson said, frankly.

Cooper stared at him as if he'd lost his mind. "Okay, I get it, she tore you up, I know that. But, man, you have got to move on."

"I'm going to call that number after you leave. I like the part on the ad that said, *absolutely* no romance involved. I don't know what made her put such strong wording like that in her ad but as far as I'm concerned it is her main selling point."

"Fine," Cooper grumbled. "Whatever it takes, just as long as you call. April will thank you."

Carson didn't want his daughter to thank him, he just wanted to do the right thing for her. She was his only reason for doing this. If it were up to him, the house was just fine the way it was. Since his ex-wife had run off a little over two years ago, he hadn't had much appetite for decorations. He'd walked out of the house he'd shared with Missy and barely took his clothes and a few sticks of furniture. He'd tried hard to wipe the slate clean of everything about Missy other than his baby girl. The thing was, he knew most of that came from a sense of betrayal he felt—and anger. He knew good and well it was time to start trying to let some of that go. No matter what Missy had done to him, she was the mother of his sweet, growing girl and he had to try to deal with her in a way that would help April have as normal a life as possible. He was thankful every day that he had custody of April. But sad for April that Missy hadn't even wanted it.

He pushed it all to the back of his thoughts as he led the way to the bull. It was time to talk business. And in two hours, it would be time to pick April up from the babysitter's. The fact she was turning five was craziness to him. She was growing up at the speed of light.

And she was the light of his world.

He'd make the call. It was time to make sure she had everything she needed to flourish. At least everything in his power to give her and hope that made up for the things he couldn't give her.

Bella Reese slowed as she saw the entrance to Carson Andrews's ranch on the outskirts of Bride, Texas. It hadn't been a bad drive, only two hours because her condo was on the outskirts of Fort Worth and not in the heart of the city or on the far side. When she'd received the call from the divorced father three days ago, she'd been intrigued by his request.

Since opening her new business six months earlier, she'd been moderately busy. Which was a blessing. But instead of helping decorate homes for clients, creating a warm and happy environment like she'd dreamed she would be doing, she'd been hosting business events. They paid the bills but so far had not satisfied the deep-rooted desire to help someone actually warm up their home. Carson Andrews's call had sent a shaft of joy ringing through her when he'd explained in not so many words that his little girl was turning five soon and he wanted to turn his house into a home, and do whatever she thought to make it a great place for his growing daughter. And he thought while she was at it, maybe she could help him with the birthday party plans.

Oh joy, oh joy! Bella had agreed to the job and after ending the call, she'd literally danced around her condo she was so excited. She was going to make this the best home Mr. Andrews and April had ever seen. For that privilege and the price he was paying her, the two-hour drive back and forth was well worth it. Truth be told, she would have taken the job for less, just to have the satisfaction of doing what she longed to do. It would also help her portfolio but that was less important to her than the satisfaction element.

She really needed the feeling of fulfillment that something like this could give her.

She needed it more than anyone close to her understood or knew.

It was a short drive up the red dirt road. The barn

came into view first and off to the side, the house. But it was the man riding the horse in the round pen off the side of the barn who had her attention. He sat straight in his saddle and had the horse backing up and then turning several quick circles, stirring up dirt as the cowboy expertly road out the quick spin. The two moved as one and she almost ran off the drive watching man and horse. Her tires hit a bump and she realized too late that she'd been distracted too long as she drove her car into the corner post of the fence.

She yanked the wheel and slammed on the brake. But it wasn't in time to save the fence or the front fender of her car as she crashed into the solid corner post with a jolting thud.

She gasped. Her heart thundered as she stared out the window at what she'd done.

This was not the way to make a good first impression.

Carson saw the car just as it scraped its front fender along the corner post of his entrance fence, knocking it slightly crooked while doing far more damage to the small cranberry-toned sedan. He'd set that post himself and knew it wasn't budging much. The metal fender, on the other hand, did not fare as well.

Dismounting, he led the colt over and tied it to the post. Then he opened the gate and strode across the gravel toward the accident. His first thought was that something had happened to the driver to cause him or her to hit the post. After all, how could you not see the thick post that was nearly the size of a telephone pole?

The door opened before he reached the car. A woman climbed out and stared at the car, her hands on slim hips. She spun toward him as he reached her.

"I am so sorry," she gasped, waving a hand toward the fence. "I cannot believe I did this."

He halted beside the post as the woman's alarmed apple-green eyes slammed into him. "I can't believe you did it either," he said, because it was the truth. "What happened? But more important, are you okay?"

She was pretty, with thick, dark hair and a gentle look to her features that gave the first impression of a gentle soul…but then again, he knew very well that looks could be deceiving.

"I'm fine. Just fine." Her mouth dropped open again as she stared at the leaning post. "I am so very sorry. I was watching you, I mean, I was driving up the drive and I glanced over and saw you and the horse spinning and I, well, I…" She halted and turned practically fire-engine red. "I mean, I forgot to look at the road and took out your pole."

He laughed. He couldn't help it. "Haven't you ever seen a cowboy on a horse before?"

"Yes. I just got caught up in how smooth the maneuver looked. It was beautiful. It really was. But still, I did this." She looked from him to the pole to the car and she cringed.

"I can tell you that the pole will live. I feel worse for your car." He was also glad April was at the babysitter's.

"Your daughter—I could have hit your daughter," she gasped again, looking not just alarmed but horrified. Her hand went to her mouth. "I can't even think about that. I am not normally so careless. I'll pay for damages and promise you it won't happen again. I am so sorry."

Carson appreciated her concern. He had been expecting Bella Reese and he decided this must be her. "Look, April's fine. She's at the babysitter's. Let's not go that direction with what could have happened. I don't take you as being the careless type, so it's all fine. You must be Bella Reese."

She took a deep breath and nodded. Then she held out her hand. "I'm Bella, and this isn't normally my way of making a good first impression."

He smiled. "You've made an entrance, that's for certain. But you've made a good impression in some ways. You cared. Just the alarm on your face shows me that. So it's fine. Knock down another post and then my impression of you will shift." He enjoyed watching the expression on her face relax. He took her hand; his pulse bolted into overdrive as he felt her fingers wrapped around his. Her beautiful eyes collided into his and he saw her awareness in the emerald depths. He released her hand like it was a sizzling pan.

She pulled hers back at nearly the same instant and he had to fight not to take a step away from her. As if that would stop the sudden and powerful awareness of Bella Reese as a woman.

How long had it been since that feeling had hit him?

He wasn't going there and slammed the door on that thought.

He rammed his hands on his hips and stared at her fender for a moment. "I'm not sure you'll be able to drive back to Fort Worth. We better make sure it didn't mess up anything with the impact."

"Okay, but I'm so sorry, this was not in the plan. I'm here to do a job for you. Not cause you problems in the middle of your workday."

"It'll be fine." He moved past her and squeezed into the driver's seat of the small car. He felt like a sardine in a matchbox. *How did women drive these cars?* "Stand back and I'll move it into the yard and make sure it's handling right."

"Sure, thank you."

He looked up at her and saw a hint of a smile at the corners of her mouth.

"You laughing at my situation? This car size should be outlawed."

She seemed to relax as a hesitant smile bloomed. "I'm not meaning to laugh at your expense but you are a car full."

"To put it mildly," he drawled, suddenly not thinking about his situation. He could barely pull his gaze off the way she looked, standing there and looking down at him. She was gorgeous-and he needed to be thinking that like he needed a swift kick in the gut by his horse. "Move back," he snapped and yanked his thoughts back to where they needed to be.

She immediately stepped back.

He slammed the door and moved the car forward. "What is wrong with you," he muttered as he drove the car to the house. Something scraped against the tire and he stopped. The fender would have to be worked on before she could drive the car. He took a moment inside the car to get his head together. Bella Reese was pretty, seemed nice and sincere. She was here to do a job and the fact that he was reacting to her like a cowpoke on his first date was ridiculous. He scowled as he pushed open the door and managed to get himself to a standing position without having to crawl out of the car and then stand up.

She had followed him and stood waiting for him to regain his upright posture.

He saw the twinkle in her eyes and reminded himself again that he wasn't interested. He straightened his hat. "You're going to have to have that fender pulled out. It's rubbing against your tire and will probably give you a blowout."

Her forehead crinkled above thoughtful eyes. "So, I'll need a body shop. Or a wrecker service. I'll have to get an estimate for my insurance. Probably rent a car. Does Bride have a rental car place?"

"No car rental but Bud Cramer can fix it and he can tow you if it needs to be towed. He's good."

"Okay, if you'll excuse me, I'll call the insurance and get this settled and then we can talk about the job you've hired me to do. I truly apologize for all of this."

He cocked his head. "Relax, I'm fine. I'll go

unsaddle my horse while you make your calls and I'll meet you on the deck. You're welcome to talk up there if you want."

"Thanks, Mr. Andrews."

"Carson. I'm not much on formality."

"Carson, then. And I'm Bella," she said and headed toward the house.

He strode back across the stretch of grass and gravel to the round pen. This scenario was already looking like more than he bargained for. Then again, she hadn't meant to nearly take down the fence or crunch her car. And he was suddenly wondering whether she seemed to have the same effect on all her clients that she'd had on him. Maybe there was a real strong reason she'd put that disclaimer in her ad. One thing was certain: he would get himself back on track and sternly remind himself that this was a strictly business proposition, just like her ad said.

He reminded himself as he unbuckled the saddle and pulled it off his horse that he wasn't interested anyway.

Not now, not ever again.

Cowoys of Ransom Creek Seires
Her Cowboy Hero (Book 1)
Bride for Hire (Book 2)
Cooper (Book 3)
Shane (Book 4)
Vance (Book 5)
Drake (Book 6)
Brice (Book 7)

HER TEXAS COWBOY

New Horizon Ranch, Book One

CHAPTER ONE

"Get in there, you ornery hunk of steaks," Maddie Rose gritted out through clamped teeth while thrusting all of her weight into pushing the cattle trailer's rear gate closed. A hard task since her hundred twenty pounds didn't hold up against Buford's two-thousand-pound bulk. Needless to say, despite all of her shoving and pushing. Despite all of her exertion. Buford's big, hairy rump hadn't budged even an inch! Nope, there it was—hanging out over the back end of the trailer.

Firmly in the way of the latch.

"C'mon, only a few more inches," she coaxed, pushing, giving it everything she had. But the bull wasn't buying it. He didn't budge.

"*Arrrg,*" she growled, frustration nearly getting the better of her.

This should have been a piece of cake, an easy load-up. Ha!

Bull-headed Buford messed that up deciding he

wanted off rather than on.

Just Maddie's luck.

And what was new about that? "*Nothing,*" she grumbled.

She wasn't a whiner, but there was no getting around the hard truth that most things in her life hadn't come easy. She'd been fighting for survival since the moment of her existence, a sickly baby only a few weeks old at best estimation, found alone, sitting in a car seat. Yup, just sitting on the steps of the post office like she belonged there.

Obviously, she didn't belong anywhere.

Maybe before that, but unlike most people Maddie had no recollection, no records, nothing. As far as her life record went, she hadn't existed until that day in the post office when she was found.

If she'd been a whiner, she wouldn't have made it.

No, Maddie was a survivor so she'd grown used to days like today. But it sure was getting old.

Buford's attitude was a sharp reminder she'd better not get comfortable with the good fortune that had recently come her way.

Owner.

The thought dazzled her. Like a beautiful sparkly gift under the Christmas tree that she knew had to belong to someone else...and yet it was hers.

She really was part owner of this magnificent New Horizon ranch. An amazing cattle ranch sitting on the outskirts of Mule Hollow, the most embracing little town she'd ever known. For a gal with her past, raised in an orphanage and then the foster care system, this homey community was as close to family as she'd ever gotten.

But she felt like an impostor.

"What had C.C. been thinking when he made me an heir?" The question plagued her since the reading of the will two months ago. The day it was revealed that her boss--God rest his sweet soul--had left his ranch to five employees: four cowboys and her.

She could understand why he'd leave her four amazing partners a share. After all, he had no children of his own, and these men had been here on the ranch for years, despite not being much older than her. They were cowboys who'd had a bond and a dedication to C.C., and they loved the ranch. She'd noticed it from the first day she'd walked onto the premises two years ago. They deserved the gift.

But why her? Had he felt sorry for her?

It wasn't as if she went around telling everyone her past. She told no one. But intuitive C.C. had guessed some facts during a conversation once.

Sympathy was the only valid reason she could come up with that she was here.

The very thought soured her stomach as life-long insecurities ran rampant inside her head. Despite those insecurities she was still an owner, and she was determined that she'd earn this gift if it was the last thing she did.

Teeth grinding down hard, she met the ill-tempered

glare of the bull. Her palms went slick on the sun-warmed metal of the trailer gate. Her insides tensed. But she'd had enough.

Digging her boots into the dirt, Maddie refused to give up or to run away. Letting the bull get the better of her was not the way to prove herself.

Working harder, accomplishing more, being competent and reliable...that was how she became deserving.

For the first time in her life, she'd been given a shot at something big. It didn't matter that she didn't deserve it. She was going to do her fair share to see that her former boss never looked down from heaven and regretted the faith he'd shown in giving her this opportunity. She'd already decided that any dream she'd had prior to the reading of that will was going on hold. There would be plenty of time for them later.

Buford snorted, setting Maddie instantly on alert. He never did anything he didn't want to do, and Maddie knew the ornery bull could make mincemeat out of her if he chose.

He chose. One powerful kick sent the gate slamming into Maddie. A scream ripped from her as the bone crunching impact knocked her off her feet. Flying backwards like a ragdoll she slammed into the pipe fence. The hit was immediately followed by the heavy, steel gate. Pain exploded everywhere, glazing everything over as it seared through her, dazing her.

Got to stay on your feet.

The gate swung away from her, and instinct had Maddie clawing, grasping for its rungs.

Stay off the ground or be trampled.

Buford kicked the gate again. This time, all Maddie's breath whooshed from her, her lungs locked up—the impact so excruciating she hit the ground instantly.

Right in Buford's pathway.

She landed face first in the dirt, and her mouth filled with foul-tasting grit. Fighting for breath, she couldn't help herself. She was helpless. A flashback to her childhood crowded her mind.

Wheezing, she willed herself to move. To breathe.

But as she'd been unable to help herself all those years ago when she was a sickly, abandoned baby, she was helpless now.

Suddenly, boots attached to denim-clad legs thudded to the ground between her and Buford.

"Yah," yelled the cowboy, planting himself directly in the line of danger as the bull bolted from the trailer like a runaway tank.

Where the cowboy had come from, Maddie didn't know, but from her position, he looked like a gift dropped straight from heaven.

"Go on, now," he yelled, then stomped and waved his arms—held his ground. Buford cut sharply to the right, away from Maddie.

Though her lungs still burned with the need for air, relief surged through her watching the cowboy herd the bull away from her and into the holding pen. Within moments he returned and dropped to his knees beside her.

"Here you go," he drawled, easing her to her side. "Try to relax. The breathing will get easier. Come on, now go easy."

She struggled to relax. He was right, after a few more inhales the breaths did come easier, though there was a sharp edge to each breath if she inhaled too deeply. "Thank. You," she managed, giving him a weak smile.

He didn't smile back. Concern etched his rugged, handsome face. "Glad I was here. How are you feeling now?"

Maddie's pulse fluttered. She was mesmerized by his penetrating indigo eyes. Flustered, she yanked her gaze off her gorgeous rescuer and rubbed her ribs, wincing. "Like I've been kicked by a two-thousand-pound bull."

His soft chuckle sank over her like warm honey.

"You may have broken some ribs," he said kindly, then demanded. "What were you doing out here by yourself in the first place?"

"Loading a bull," she retorted, humiliated by the entire pitiful ordeal and the fact he'd witnessed it. This cowboy probably thought she was some greenhorn who didn't know beans about bulls or cattle.

Needing more control, she struggled to sit up without groaning. Honestly, she was feeling better—but who wouldn't? Her cowboy rescuer would make any woman forget she'd been almost stomped to a pulp by a bull, even her.

And that those eyes of his were lethal weapons.

The guy was gorgeous. Even oxygen-deprived and in pain as she'd been, she'd realized that immediately. Touchable dark hair curled from beneath his straw hat and enhanced his firm, chiseled jaw. His high cheekbones underlined those penetrating, strength-filled, blue eyes.

He flashed an enticing crooked grin. "You're one tough lady, Maddie Rose."

Maddie got hung-up on that smile, suddenly thinking about long, slow kisses... There was an understandable delay in her fogged brain relaying the message that he knew her name.

And she'd never met him. She knew because she would have remembered him if she'd met him *anytime* in her entire life. And yet, she realized there was something slightly familiar about him.

"Have we met?" she asked, as dawning hit her dazed brain and she saw the resemblance. "Wait, you're Cliff Masterson, Rafe's twin brother. The bull rider." Rafe was one of her ranch partners and a good friend.

"Some nights. Some nights I eat more dirt than you just did." His expression was a mixture of humor and ire, one that made him look more like his brother than he had so far. Rafe had said they weren't identical by a long shot. He'd been right.

They were both dark-haired, good-looking and with

similar face shapes and body builds, but other than the occasional similarity of expressions, a person would never mistake them for twins.

She relaxed, some. "Rafe said you were coming, but I thought it wasn't until next week."

His left cheek twitched. "My plans changed."

She'd caught the way his expression tightened and pain briefly dulled his eyes. "Oh—"

"How about we get you up to the house?" he asked, and before she could answer or even nod, he'd moved behind her and in an instant his strong arms slipped around her, gently lifting her up.

Momentarily all pain disappeared. His purely masculine scent wrapped around her, drawing her like a hummingbird to sugar water. She fought the overwhelming urge to lean into him.

"Lean on me," he said as if he could read her mind.

Ha! Like she needed any encouragement. Even the sharp pains shooting from her ribs overrode the initial shock of his touch, Maddie's awareness of the man stunned her.

She didn't let men get too close. Held them at bay. And even though she got lonely and hoped one day she'd have the guts to change that, this kind of reaction had never been a problem.

Never happened.

She chalked it up to the fault of the ordeal she'd just gone through.

It didn't matter anyway. Not right now. Finding the guts to knock down her emotional barriers. To risk her heart for her dream of falling in love and having the family she longed for—that dream was on hold for now.

She had other priorities. Like not flubbing up any more. To prove to herself that she was deserving of this gift.

Needing a hero to ride to her rescue was not the way to do it.

CHAPTER TWO

Cliff Masterson's stomach clenched thinking about how close Maddie had come to being trampled by the huge bull. If he'd arrived at the ranch a moment later, he wouldn't have seen Maddie fly through the air and hit the pipe fence like a sack of concrete. He wouldn't have heard her scream when the trailer gate slammed her. And worse, he wouldn't have seen her crumple to the ground in the path of Buford's hooves.

He hadn't thought he was going to make it to her in time.

When he'd scaled the fence and landed between her and the crazy bull, his pulse was exploding. Even now, his heart hammered and his mouth went dry thinking about her being crushed beneath the bull. What if he hadn't shown up?

"You're doing great," he encouraged, squeezing her shoulder gently as they eased their way toward the ranch house. "Hopefully those ribs are only bruised and not broken. But I speak from experience--there isn't too much difference. Bruised ribs are as painful as broken ribs. At least in the beginning. Broken take a lot longer to heal though."

She huffed out a shaky laugh. "I guess you would know about that, being a bull rider."

"More than I care to think about. Think about something else to put the pain out of your mind." He glanced down at her, and her pale caramel hair tickled his nose. She felt slight in his arms, and he found himself willing her to look back up at him with those huge green eyes. Eyes that had zapped him like a hotwire the moment he'd rolled her over and she'd planted them on him.

He never felt anything like the electric surge that had arched instantly through him, or the protective instincts still driving him where she was concerned.

He forced himself not to think too closely about his reaction to her. He knew full well that he had issues fogging his head right now. Until a week ago, he'd thought he had his life figured out. Had grown good at ignoring his past.

He'd thought he'd left it behind the day he and Rafe had struck out on their own when they were barely seventeen.

But now his dad was dead.

And for reasons he wasn't sure about, Cliff was now questioning everything he'd ever thought about himself.

"That was really stupid of me," Maddie said, her disgust-filled words yanking Cliff out of the past. "I should never have gotten in there until he was far enough into the trailer."

"True," he said, not wanting to make her feel worse. But the danger she'd put herself in was still too fresh on his mind. "I certainly didn't expect a rooky mistake like that from you, not after the description Rafe gave me."

The minute the words were out of his mouth, he knew he'd said something wrong. If he'd been hoping for her to look at him, mission accomplished. Her head jerked back against his shoulder, her expression guarded she stared up at him, her gaze narrowed suspiciously.

"Why were y'all talking about me?"

Their faces were mere inches away, so close he could see the deeper flecks of green dotting the huge pools of emerald. His mind went blank looking into their luscious depths. The sudden desire to lower his head and kiss her nearly overwhelmed him.

He swallowed hard. *What's wrong with me?* Instead of getting a grip, his gaze wandered from her tempting lips over her jawline to the reckless beating pulse at the base of her throat.

Whoa there, hotshot, he warned himself. He hadn't come here to get infatuated with his brother's partner. He'd come to figure out what he wanted out of life. For a man who'd always thought he'd known the answer to that, it had come as quite a blow when he'd realized that he might have been running from his past instead of reaching for a dream.

"Don't get all riled up," he said, glad they'd made it to the house. He used the time it took to cross the patio and get inside to try and get his thoughts on track. Once they were in, he headed across the large kitchen to the table, where he pulled out a chair for her.

She eased onto the seat and looked up at him. "Well?" she prompted, her pretty mouth twisted into a small frown.

Obviously she was prickly about being talked about. "Rafe talks about all of his ranch partners. He says y'all are all good at your jobs. Says you in particular are one of the best cowboys he's ever seen despite you being female and all," he teased.

"Oh." Her brows dipped, and her cheeks flushed a pretty pink. "Well, I do my work."

"And then some, from what Rafe said," he offered, then planted his hands on his hips and voiced what had been eating at him from the moment he saw her flying through the air. "My question is, *why* in blue blazes were you out there loading that bull by yourself? Where is my brother and all of those partners who are supposed to be so good at their jobs?"

Sure, he'd already picked up on the fact that she felt like she could do it on her own. That didn't mean it was right.

It also didn't make it any of his business, but he'd never been the best at minding his own business when it came to females getting a raw deal. It probably was a psychological effect left over from watching his mother get a raw deal from his good for nothing dad. She'd taken it for years before her premature death when he was seventeen.

It didn't matter what it was born from. Fact was if Cliff saw a woman who needed help, he stepped in. Even if it was one like Maddie who he'd figured was too stubborn to want help. Or too independent to ask for it.

He told himself he should back off, not let himself get any more involved than needed, but that was Cliff's trouble. He tended to acted on instinct in situations like this.

And since learning his dad was dead, he'd come to realize his instincts were off-kilter.

Looking into Maddie Rose's luminous green eyes, every protective instinct he had went on high alert.

But from the jut of her chin and the tension filling the room, he figured she was about to tell him and his instincts to back off. However, that wasn't happening, because the way he saw it, his brother or one of the other cowboys should have been here helping her out. And he aimed to know why she'd been in that pen attempting to load that bull alone.

He'd been the one to witness her nearly get trampled by a bull. That invested him in this as far as he was concerned. After all, he'd have been the one rushing her to the hospital if he'd arrived any later than he had.

Yeah, he wanted to know why...and he felt like he

had a right.

* * *

"Because Buford is due at the auction today by five, and I'm the one taking him, that's why," Maddie said, irritated at her reactions to the man. Still stunned that the instant he'd wrapped his arm around her, all coherent thought had abandoned her.

The clock on the solid brick wall beside the kitchen table ticked a few beats into the silence as Cliff held her gaze. She was glad there was a little distance between them at last. Hopefully she'd start thinking clearer again.

She rubbed her neck and wondered what his story was. Wondered what had caused that shadow in his eyes moments ago.

All things she didn't need to be concerned with.

If there was one thing her life had taught her, it was to keep her guard up. The few times she'd relented in the past she'd regretted it. Maybe one day she'd find the courage to risk being hurt one more time, if it meant she could have the family she always dreamed of. But that was on hold for now while she gave everything she had to this ranch.

Besides, she told herself, she'd reacted so strongly toward Cliff out of a sense of gratefulness. She hated to think what would have happened if he hadn't shown up when he had.

"It's not safe," he said, at last. Frowning. "For

anyone. Especially a woman."

She bristled. "I can take care of myself."

"Hey, I'm concerned for you. And glad I happened by or you'd be out there right now, hurt and alone with a one-ton bull tap dancing all over you. And I for one don't like the thought of that." His voice dropped an octave on the last part, softened enough to cause her heart to knot dangerously. Suddenly he knelt beside her, and before she knew what he was doing, his warm hand splayed open-palmed over her left rib cage.

She jumped, gasped, at the intimacy of his touch.

"Easy there. I'm just testing your ribs."

Her heart knotted tighter. "Okay," Maddie quipped, trying for nonchalance, trying hard not to be affected by his touch and nearness. But she was.

Her breath warbled when he pressed gently while his gaze searched hers. Held. She bit her lip as she held his azure gaze, feeling as if she were freefalling.

"Breathe in and tell me if it hurts. Any sharp pains?"

Only at his urging did she realize she'd been holding her breath since he'd spread his long fingers over her ribs. Trying not to focus on his touch, she inhaled slowly. "It's okay. No sharp pains." He moved his hand to the other side.

"And this side?"

"Fine," she said tightly.

From his kneeling position, she had a close up view of the easy smile that spread across his face, crinkling the edges of his eyes.

"That's great news. You still may want to see a doc." He stood and moved to the kitchen counter where he started prowling through her cabinets. "Do you have some painkillers for the soreness that's certain to set in?"

"In that cabinet." She pointed him in the right direction and watched him locate it. She was more than a little aware that the warmth of his touch still lingered and her heart was still behaving oddly.

After being directed to the glasses he brought two pills to her with a glass of water.

"These will help."

"Thanks." She was grateful to have them. Though she was beginning to feel more like herself, she knew even if her ribs weren't broken, a tough few days were ahead for her. She didn't want to think about the pain, so she would have to find a way to make it through. She was good at that. She'd make it.

"I'm sure Rafe is going to be happy to see you." She knew they weren't real close. At least that was what she'd gathered when she'd overheard Rafe talking to two of her other partners, Dalton and Chase. From what he'd said, Cliff basically lived on the road, zigzagging across the country from one bull riding event or rodeo to the other. And honing his skills in between. He hadn't held onto his spot as a Pro Bull Riding favorite because he was bad or undedicated.

She didn't want any part of that kind of lifestyle and didn't understand it, but she had to admire his dedication.

"They should be back before evening," she said.

"They're branding cattle on the far side of the ranch. It's a big job."

"I'm in no hurry. You're a whole lot prettier than my brother."

Maddie knew she looked a mess. Her honey-colored hair was stringing loose from her ponytail. One long pale strand hung at the edge of her eyes, tickling her cheek.

She found herself smiling at him anyway. "No doubt about it. You are definitely Rafe's brother. You're as full of nonsense as he is."

That crooked white grin flashed across his face again and tickled her insides. He'd relaxed against the counter, one booted foot crossed over the other, his arms loosely crossed.

"Darlin', I'm only stating the facts. You do own a mirror, don't you?"

His drawl and the way he called her darlin' was pure Texas. And that grin and those twinkling eyes, well, it was no wonder her pulse kicked in again, even despite knowing it didn't mean anything. It probably came natural, especially to a cowboy used to laying on the charm for the cameras and crowds he encountered at the Pro events he participated in.

Faking an unaffected air, she shot him a look of mild disbelief. "Does that line work for you most of the time?"

"What line? You having a little dirt on your face doesn't change the facts."

She laughed, surprising herself. He was good. Maddie had been living among cowboys for several years now, and she'd heard her fair share of the slow-drawled pickup lines.

"Right." She curbed the laugh. "Well, this dirty-faced cowgirl's got to try and load up a bull." Her ribs rebelled as she eased to a standing position. She ignored them.

"Whoa. You aren't serious?" Stepping in front of her, he blocked her path to the door.

"Yes. Now that I've caught my breath and can tell nothings broken, it's time to get back to work. I've got a job to finish."

"But your ribs?"

"They'll be fine. Thanks to you and that painkiller you gave me, I'll be able to get Buford to the sale. I can still make it."

"But--" His eyes flashed fire as Maddie sidestepped him and made it to the door. "This isn't right. Rafe needs to get back here and take care of this."

Maddie swung back around, instantly regretting it as sharp knives of pain stabbed her good. "Hold on, cowboy. This is *my* job, and I always finish my jobs."

"Your ribs could be cracked."

"We've been over this already. You know perfectly well that other than wrapping my ribs, there is nothing the doc can do for me. If it was you, you would already be out there loading that bull. Don't even try to deny it. I'm no different. I have to do this." He had no idea how much she meant that statement. Her conscience wouldn't let her slack up.

His expression tightened as if he wanted to deny it

and couldn't because it was true. "Right." It was a frustrated growl.

Ignoring the nagging pain, she went out onto the back porch and tromped from the patio a little more forcefully than necessary, punishing herself unduly.

Cliff caught up to her. "If you have to do this, then I'll load the blasted bull. You sit down."

She didn't like his tone, but she could actually understand his frustration. He had witnessed her in a terrible situation that could have been a total disaster.

"Look, I'm very grateful you showed up when you did. I truly am. I can't thank you enough. But if you keep bossing me around, we're going to lock horns."

His brown brows dipped in consternation--or aggravation--she didn't really care. At least he was listening.

"You're as stubborn as Rafe said you were."

"You better believe it. So either help or leave. But back off for certain."

And there it was, one of two reasons why Maddie Rose was still a single woman. Men, dad-blame their hides, might *think* she was beautiful. Might *think* they could control her. But they always had a rude awakenin', because Maddie was the driver now. She'd been at the wheel of her life ever since she'd walked out of the last foster home when she was ten days away from being eighteen.

And that was the way it was staying.

Since the day she was born, other folks had dictated

every aspect of her life. And she wouldn't ever let that happen again.

Ignoring the pang of regret, she undid the chain on the holding pen gate and let herself in. Cliff could follow if he wanted. She didn't care one way or the other.

He followed.

Maddie's heart jumped in her chest when he winked at her, tipped his hat, then headed toward Buford with the confidence of a man who knew what he was doing.

Watching him saunter across the pen, Maddie's mouth went dry and a shudder swept through her. Every instinct she had told her there was something about this cowboy that might be more dangerous to her than Buford, the pig-headed bull.

CHAPTER THREE

Despite the pain she had to be in, Maddie helped get Buford back into the loading chute by waving one arm and holding her ribs with the other when he ran her way. Cliff had to battle the urge to hoist the spitfire into his arms and carry her out of the pen kicking and screaming if need be. He decided the best course of action was to help her.

The woman acted driven. Like if she didn't get her job done, she'd miss out on making the National Rodeo Finals or something. It didn't make sense to him. He and Rafe might not have spent a lot of time together over the last few years because he was on the road all the time, but he knew Rafe wouldn't make Maddie feel like her loading this bull was a do or die deal.

So what was up with her? It was just a bull.

"There you go, mission accomplished," he said, closing the trailer's gate shut with Buford safely inside and Maddie safely on the outside.

Maddie stood with her hands on her slim, jean-clad hips and watched him, green flames flickering in her eyes. It was like she knew she needed help but she didn't want it.

"You like taking control, don't you?" It wasn't a question but a statement.

He hiked a brow at her. "Funny, I was about to say the same thing about you. I'd say we have something in common."

Her eyes softened, the fire faded as some of the fight went out of her. "Look, this isn't easy for me. I'm not normally so careless. Thanks for loading Buford."

Either she didn't like accepting help at all. Or she didn't like it from him. Either way, saying thank you was obviously hard for her.

"You're welcome." He went to the truck's passenger door and opened it for her. "Hop in., I'm driving."

"No, that's okay. I'll take it from here."

"I'll drive you and the bull to the auction, Maddie. All you have to do is show me the way."

She didn't move. "Can you not hear?"

He chuckled. "I have selective hearing. Do we really have to go through this again? You're injured whether you want to admit it or not, and I'm not about to let you do this alone. You warned me earlier to back off or we were going to lock horns. Consider our horns locked. Either you hop in and I drive, or I'll take the keys and your bull won't make it to the sale today."

"Of all the nerve," she huffed, moving past him to

ease into the passenger's seat.

The Dodge had running boards that came in handy, making it easier for her to climb into the cab than if it had been his truck. She kept one arm wrapped across her ribs, and he caught the strain in her expression. She was still in a heap of pain and trying to hide it…or ignore it. He laid his hand on her waist to assist if he could.

Fiery eyes met his and had him fighting the sudden, strong urge to kiss her. Not a good idea on any fronts, but especially now. He'd just met her, for one, and he didn't figure her ribs could handle the pain when she took a swing at him.

"So, when are you leaving?" she snapped, sliding into the leather seat.

He grinned. "Trying to get rid of me so quick?"

"I'll buy you a tank of gas if you need me to spell it out any clearer."

"Rafe didn't mention it?"

"You are not a topic of conversation your brother and I discuss."

He chuckled. "Well, for your information, I'm here for a little while. I'm thinking of buying a place in Mule Hollow. Time to put down some roots."

Her face went slack as he closed the door. He jogged around and slid behind the wheel and glanced at her. Yup, she still wore that oh-no-tell-me-it-ain't-true expression of shock and dismay.

"Makes you nervous, doesn't it?"

She went all prune faced. Not her best look, but

somehow she managed to pull it off. "I don't care what you do. It's a free country." Reaching for her seatbelt, she gasped when she couldn't twist her torso to grab it from its dock beside her shoulder.

"Here. Let me." Leaning over, he reached across her to grab it. Neither of them said anything as he made sure it wasn't too tight before securing it.

He hated she was hurting and didn't like having to push her around like he'd been doing, but he couldn't figure any other way to make her let him help her.

He headed the truck and trailer out of the loading area and the endless, high dollar pipe fencing. They circled around past the massive tan and red trimmed metal barn and then on past the ranch house that was a showcase of sandstone rock and redwood logs. New Horizon ranch was a showplace. From what Rafe had told him, C.C. Calvert had been worth a bundle, and this ranch had been one of his hobbies, but he'd loved it.

Hobby or not, the man hadn't made the money he'd made without knowing how to put people in place who could maintain his hobbies and businesses in his absence. For the ranch, that had been Rafe and his partners.

"This is a beautiful place," he said as they drove down the fence-lined lane leading from the house to the black top road. "A little bigger than what I'm looking for though." He shot her a grin, hoping to ease the tension that filled the cab.

She didn't say anything, instead looked like she was mulling over when would be a good time to push him out of the truck. He had to smile at that thought.

"Which way am I going?" he asked when they reached the road. She nodded left and he eased the truck out on the road and pressed the gas.

He slid a peek at Maddie, curious about what her story was. "It's pretty country around here." They'd gone about five miles down the road heading away from the direction of Mule Hollow. This was prime cattle country. Right on the edge of Texas hill country, it was a good combination of flat land mixed with the rolling hills and deep ravines that made it both interesting and beautiful. He'd seen a lot of country over the last ten years. While not as breathtaking as the Colorado vistas or some of the other places he'd been, there was something about this area that spoke to him. From the moment Rafe had settled here almost five years ago, he'd said it was a good place to make a life. Cliff figured it was time he at least gave it a try.

He was a thirty-year-old man who'd spent the last ten years moving fast and light. Everything he owned fit into a gear box that held his bull riding gear and a large duffle bag. He didn't live so sparse because he couldn't afford anything more. He lived that way because he had goals and dreams, and riding bulls filled the empty holes in his life.

At least that was what he'd always thought. Told himself. Believed.

Since he'd learned last week that his dad was dead, something had snapped inside of him, and he'd suddenly begun to question everything he'd ever believed about himself. He wanted to chalk it up to the fact that it was getting easier and easier for him to get injured. The thirty-year-old body of a professional bull rider wasn't as resilient as that of a twenty-two-year-old. He wanted to chalk it up to the fact that after ten years of hard work and dedication he was road weary.

But he knew that wasn't true.

Sure he'd always had a plan for when it came time for him to hang up his spurs. But he'd kept putting it off over the years. Now, suddenly it almost seemed like he couldn't make it happen soon enough.

And that sudden change of heart had slammed him like Buford had slammed Maddie the moment he'd learned his dad was finally dead.

Funny thing was, he'd already planned on making the trip to Mule Hollow and checking out land. He'd already put the wheels in motion before the call.

But the call, it had changed everything.

Suddenly starting his business of breeding bulls, warriors for the circuit couldn't happen fast enough. He was still sorting through why this change had come over him.

"Do you know of any small, good places around here for sale?" he asked, needing space between him and his thoughts.

"Me?"

"I was thinking since you live here, you might know of a place or two."

He glanced back at the road, but out of the corner of his eye, he caught her biting her lower lip.

"What, um--" she cleared her throat, "--sort of facilities do you need? What plans do you have for it? It'd help to know."

He shot her a grateful look, and she gave him a small, not-quite-certain smile.

"Bulls. I'm going to raise bucking bulls for the industry. I have some young stock housed at different breeders across the country, and I figure it's time to gather them all together and get down to business. And now that Rafe is going to settle here for good since being named partner in the ranch, I'd like to be near him." It was true.

"That's nice," she said, but didn't look exactly thrilled at the prospect of him hanging around.

He realized that he, on the other hand, found the prospect of being around her intriguing. He laughed. "Don't look all gloomy. I promise not to come over every day and fire you up."

Her cheeks flamed. "I wasn't worried about that."

But they both knew that had been exactly what she'd been thinking about.

He had things about his past that he needed to come to terms with, to try and make sense of...but for reasons he was suddenly interested in figuring out, getting to know Maddie Rose put a whole other spin on things.

CHAPTER FOUR

Maddie spent an hour soaking in a sea salt bath. The rose scent lingered on her skin as she eased into soft sweat pants and an oversized, poppy-colored top. When she and Cliff finally made it home from dropping off Buford, she'd been worn out and nearly doubled over from the pain radiating through her back and ribs. She hurt everywhere.

Despite the tension that still stretched between them like a thick rubber band, tensing and giving, but threatening to snap at any given moment, he'd helped her from the truck, and she'd leaned on him as they entered the house.

She'd barely pointed him in the direction of the upstairs guest room before shuffling through the lower level to her room down the hall from the kitchen.

The soak and more painkillers had eased some of her discomfort. Her stomach growled, reminding her that she hadn't eaten since grabbing a couple of pieces of bacon that morning. But though she felt better, she did not feel like cooking. She didn't even feel like making a peanut butter sandwich.

But most of all, like a big chicken, she didn't want to run into Cliff again. Chicken was the right word, too, because she really wanted more than anything to go back in there and see if she was as attracted to him as she thought.

And if so, what was she going to do about it? She'd had to have a little talk with herself during her soak about the way she'd treated him all afternoon. And she'd had to ask the Lord to forgive her and also to help her understand why she was so affected by him. No answers had come, but it hadn't even been an hour. She should probably give the Lord a little more time than that.

Cliff was bossy and infuriating. *And gentle and caring.*

True. How could a man rub her the wrong way one minute and make her all gooey inside the next?

She'd known him all of one afternoon, so this conversation seemed premature anyway. Wasn't it?

She needed to turn her focus back to finding a way to feel deserving of owning this ranch. It was proving to be a hard thing to accept, especially after days like today. It had taken her a long time to accept God's love too, but she'd finally understood John 3:16, For God so loved the world that he gave his only begotten son. That whosoever believeth in him should have everlasting life...

For a sick kid abandoned by her parents—rejected,

unwanted for adoption and then raised in the foster care system like she'd been, it had been hard to believe that God actually cared for her. Much less loved her and gave His son for her.

She'd learned to trust God. But she was still having trouble trusting that anyone other than God would leave her something like the partnership in this ranch.

She was also having a hard time believing she could ever trust someone with her heart. Abandonment issues were tough. They were real. And they scared her to death.

Because unless she ever got past them, she would never be able to let a man get close enough to her to fall in love. And if she couldn't do that, then she'd never have the family and the white-picket-fence-happily-ever-after buried deep in her heart.

She'd never found a man who tempted her to throw caution and fear to the wind.

But Cliff Masterson was different.

As emotionally unavailable as she'd always been, her emotions had been electrified today. She stared out the window to the backyard as thoughts of how she felt when Cliff looked at her came to mind. Her skin tingled thinking about it, as if she'd been out in the cold for too long, and his warm gaze was bringing her back to life.

Someone knocked on her door.

"Maddie, I've made some dinner."

Dinner? Cliff had cooked!

Her stomach rumbled again at the thought.

"Are you awake?"

It crossed her mind to pretend she was asleep, but...he'd cooked for her. She'd *never* had a man cook something just for her. Sure, the guys took turns like she did with kitchen duty, but that was for everyone.

Unable to stop herself, she padded slowly in her bare feet across the cool tile floor and opened the door. Her heart dropped to her toes. Cliff was smiling like he was thrilled to see her.

It was too irresistible to deny. Her defenses were down already. Her pulse raced unevenly as his gaze slid over her, dropping to her bare feet. Awareness danced across her skin.

She loved the way it felt.

"You look good and relaxed. Exactly what the doctor ordered. Now he's ordering food, if you're up to it?"

"I'm starving. I skipped lunch today and barely ate breakfast. And it smells fabulous out here."

He chuckled. "Cowboy Mash. It's got a real romantic ring, doesn't it?" He stepped aside so she could move past him in the hallway. Her pulse jumped at his nearness.

"I don't know about romantic, but I'm attracted to that spicy scent." She could have said the same for him and his fresh showered scent. Instead she clamped her lips tightly shut on that and ignored the temptation to linger beside him.

As it turned out, he'd set the table out on the stone patio. C.C. had often eaten his meals out there. When she'd come to the house to report to him, they'd sit here and go over the details of the day. C.C. hadn't done a lot of business in his ranch office. Said he spent enough time in offices when he was away from the ranch.

"This is one of my favorite spots," she said, seeing the two plates of food and tall glasses of iced tea. "I can't believe you cooked."

"We have to eat. And I figured you'd probably curl up and go hungry if I didn't do something."

She laughed. "Bingo."

He pulled a chair out for her and she eased into it. Her heart hammered in her chest.

"This is one of the nicest things anyone has ever done for me." She hadn't meant to blurt that out.

A look of horror flashed across his face. "I hope not."

She laughed again. "I meant, you could have simply fixed a sandwich. Or at least left it on the stove and said dig in. There really is a nice guy behind that controlling attitude."

He sat across from her. "I'm going to ignore that remark." He lifted the lid on the pan, and the aroma instantly filled the space between them.

"Please do if it means we can eat. I'm dying over here."

"Patience, and stop trying to control me." He hiked a teasing brow, then scooped out a large portion of the pasta and meat dish onto her plate.

"Funny." She matched his raised brow with her own. Warning bells rang inside her head, but at the moment she was too hungry to heed them.

"I learned this from an old friend on the road. It's

easy to make and delicious. But then, anything with green chilies, cheese and tomatoes is going to be good in my book."

"I totally agree." And she was right. One bite proved it. Cliff could cook.

"So, how did you get mixed up with this rough group?"

"They're a great group. Like brothers to me. I--" She caught herself before she blurted out that she was a foster kid. She didn't tell anyone about her past. C.C. had figured out some of it, and she suspected knowing had spurred his decision to include her.

Cliff finished off a bite of Cowboy Mash. "So they have you fooled. But really, what brought you out here to do hard labor on the ranch? Labor you're excellent at, from what Rafe says. C.C. must have thought the same."

"I didn't feel excellent this afternoon. I felt like a beginner."

"Nah, things happen. So, what brought you here?"

He sounded genuinely interested. "I was on my way to a ranch in Corpus Christi for an interview, and the tire of my truck blew out right in front of this ranch. Your brother and Chase happened by when I was changing it. They stopped and, a little like you, they tried to take over. In the end we compromised, and then they invited me up to the ranch. Turned out C.C. was hiring. So here I am. I fell in love with the ranch and Mule Hollow. It's a wonderful community." She didn't mention how for the first time in her life she'd felt like she belonged.

Belonging was a very strong need.

Almost as strong as needing to be loved.

* * *

Two hours later, with the red glow of the sun settling on the horizon, Cliff stood out by the arena watching the horses when Rafe and Ty Calder drove into the yard. Chase Hartley and Dalton Bourne followed in a second truck pulling a trailer. The sun was disappearing and the heat of the day fading to a low simmer rather than the high boil of a Texas afternoon in July.

He'd met Rafe's partners a couple of years ago when he'd banged his shoulder up and spent a couple of weeks at the ranch with Rafe. That had been the last time he'd been to see his brother and the longest time they'd spent together since walking out of the battleground they'd called home.

Maddie hadn't been here then. He'd missed her by a month or so, if he remembered correctly.

Rafe bailed out of the truck first, a wide grin on his face. "Hey, brother!" he called, crossing in long strides to meet Cliff, giving him a hard handshake and then yanking him into a quick hug. They hadn't been around each other, but they were twin brothers and their bond remained strong.

They'd also been through a lot together. What doesn't kill you makes you stronger. And closer.

"It's been too long," Cliff said, knowing it was true as

he stepped back from their hug and grinned. "Man, it's good to see you, Rafe."

"Tell me about it, world traveler." Rafe's expression had a teasing look to it.

Chase and the others came up and greetings were exchanged. They were dust-covered, sweat-soaked and smelling of cattle.

"Y'all look like y'all've had a day of it." He shook their hands as they held them out. "I still haven't figured out what in the world y'all's boss was thinking though, leavin' y'all in charge." He chuckled.

"Believe me, we wonder the same things," Chase said. Unlike Clint, he wasn't joking. "But C.C. was a good man, and he always knew what he wanted, and he did it."

"True," Ty added, scrubbing the stubble on his lean jaw. "I have to say I've had my doubts about a couple of these fellas. Especially your brother. I don't think C.C. ever saw him rope. He hasn't gotten any better with one since you were here two years ago."

That got chuckles from the rest of the group.

"Whoa, now," Rafe warned, a grin in his voice. "I'm good with a rope, and y'all know it. It's the hopping from the horse at a dead run that had me stumbling."

Cliff knew that seven years ago when Rafe had blown his knee out, it had been hard on him. It had forced him to give up calf-roping as a sport and take up cowboy'n full time. Shutting the door on a dream wasn't ever easy, but Rafe had come to terms with it. Cliff had been lucky to have remained relatively uninjured in bull-riding. He'd been blessed to see his dream in the rodeo fulfilled for the most part.

"So, what happened?" Rafe asked. "We thought you were going to drive out to the branding and meet us there."

Cliff hiked a shoulder. "I got sidetracked. Speaking of which, I have a bone to pick with you knuckleheads. What were y'all thinking abandoning Maddie? Leaving her to load that bull by herself was a blamed bad move. If I hadn't gotten here when I did, she could have been killed."

All of them went on alert.

"What happened?" Dalton Bourne demanded first. "Is she okay?"

He quickly filled them in on the situation, and when he finished, they understood full well how he felt about the situation they'd placed Maddie in.

They all looked uncomfortable and relieved that she wasn't harmed more than she was.

Chase's serious gunmetal gray eyes locked on him. "I'm glad you were here and sorry she got hurt. But Maddie's adamant that we treat her like we treat each other. Truth is, she can load cattle with her eyes closed and her arms tied behind her back."

"True." Dalton grunted. "Still, I've never liked it. But she'd look at it as an insult if we tried to hang around and watch over her while she loads a bull. You've seen how tough she is."

Cliff saw their point. "She's tough, but still, I'd do

what I thought was best, even if it made her mad." His temperature spiked all over again thinking about seeing her going down in that pen.

"Oh, you'd have made her mad all right." Rafe chuckled along with the others as they headed toward the house. "Since you're out here and she's nowhere to be seen, I'm thinking you probably already did."

They'd reached the house, and as he said that he entered the empty kitchen, looking around for Maddie.

"She's already turned in for the night. Said she'd see y'all in the morning. And all I can say is she's something when she's mad. Those gorgeous green eyes are more beautiful than a roman candle exploding."

Four sets of eyes pinned him to the wall.

He held up his hands. "Hey, just because you idiots and all the other cowboys in Mule Hollow are blind doesn't mean I am." It was when she was calm she was the most spectacular. Over dinner he'd hardly been able to concentrate on the meal, especially when they'd gotten to talking about the ranch. Her love of it was obvious. He'd enjoyed listening to her more than he had anything in a long time.

"We know she's beautiful, but...it's Maddie." Dalton's eyes narrowed to slits. "You watch yourself with her."

"Yeah, she's off-limits," Chase snapped. He stepped up to Cliff. "She's no rodeo groupie."

The others quickly echoed his warning.

Cliff raised his hands to halt them. "Hold on. For one, I've never been into groupies. Second, I'm here scouting ranches to buy for a bull ranch, so relax."

Rafe's frown turned instantly to a smile. "You're serious?"

"I told you three weeks ago I was coming to do that."

"Yeah, but saying it and doing it are two entirely different things."

So that was why his brother hadn't said anything about him moving here. He didn't believe Cliff was going to do it.

"I'm doing it. I'm not getting any younger, and it's time for me to get the ball rolling on my future." And I like Maddie, he almost said, but caught himself. He wasn't ready to voice the interest their female partner had stirred in him. Especially after the warnings they'd issued.

"What *is* that smell?" Dalton lifted the lid on the pot sitting on the stove and breathed appreciatively letting the full saucy aroma fill the room.

That was all it took for the four of them to lay off him as they pounced on the dinner like a pack of coyotes to roadkill.

Which was exactly what Cliff had felt like there for a few minutes when they'd started warning him away from Maddie.

CHAPTER FIVE

"Ohhh, tell me I'm not dead." Maddie groaned the instant she woke up. Sprawled on her bed, she stared up at the ceiling like she had for much of the endless night. She lifted an arm, and the movement hurt all the way to her bellybutton.

Bed rest was not for her, though. Pushing herself up from the mattress, she groaned again when her ribs and all the muscles in her back seized up. She bit her lip to hold back a cry of pain.

Today was not going to be fun. Gritting her teeth, she moved toward the bathroom and a really hot shower.

Twenty minutes or so later, her muscles more relaxed from the near-blazing hot water, she moved slowly down the hall toward the kitchen. Laughter and joking filled the house, and the comforting sounds of her friends eased her pain. She also knew working her sore muscles would help as much as the camaraderie she'd have out there with them. It would help take her mind off her pain and make her feel like she was doing her fair share of the work.

Suffering in her room alone was not for Maddie.

"Are you looking at land today?"

Maddie heard Rafe's question as she rounded the corner into the kitchen. Cliff had been on her mind all night. Okay, so thinking about him helped ease her pain a few times.

Then her thoughts had crossed over into remembering how it had felt to be held in his arms, and she'd slammed the door on those thoughts. They were too dangerous to contemplate; she was already in enough pain.

Though she'd expected to see him in the kitchen this morning, she wasn't prepared for the way her pulse took off at a reckless gallop the moment those indigo eyes met hers. A sigh whispered through her as she looked at him.

Thankfully the kitchen was alive with activity even though it was only six in the morning, and she was able to focus on the activity of eggs frying and bacon sizzling in the pans. Okay, so maybe not that, since she felt like she was in the frying pan herself.

"Good morning," she said.

Rafe and Cliff were working side by side at the stove as she passed them and went straight for the coffee.

"You look better," Cliff said, drawing her gaze. He smiled, and for that brief, unrealistic moment, all was wonderful in the world.

Maddie lost her voice. His eyes crinkled at the edges, the blue warming as if he could tell he affected her so strongly.

"I feel better." She hugged her insulated coffee mug between both hands and took a sip, trying not to be affected.

She reached for a banana, ignoring the shooting pain the motion caused.

Immediately she was bombarded with questions. She lived in a huge house with four gorgeous men who were the brothers she never had. She had expected this. Still, she wasn't uncomfortable with it.

"I'm fine, everyone. Yes, my ribs are sore, but it's nothing I can't handle. Thanks to Cliff, I sustained only bruising from the pen and not stomping from Buford." She headed for the door, intent on getting her horse saddled and ready for the day before they all threw a fit and tried to stop her.

"Hang on. Where are you going?" Dalton asked.

Rafe swung around with a spatula in his hand. "Sit down." He pointed the spatula at the chair and sounded far too much like his brother.

"I'm sure y'all already have your horses saddled and loaded for the branding today, and I have a feeling mine's been conveniently left in the barn."

"Nope, no way." Cliff's scowl could have fried the bacon without a burner. Her too, for that matter.

"Maybe you need to hang loose today, Maddie." Dalton looked from her to Cliff. "We'll get the branding done. From what Cliff said, you're bruised up pretty bad."

Maddie was in no mood for this. "I'm fine. I missed

helping with the cattle yesterday."

"Yeah, but we needed Buford on the auction block, and you were the one who pulled the short straw."

That was true. Taking the old bull to the auction hadn't been something any of them had wanted to do. But she'd been the one to pull the straw, literally. After what he'd done to her, she hadn't felt so bad selling him.

"I'm fine, y'all. And I'm helping with the cattle today."

She didn't wait for further protests. They wouldn't have let bruised ribs keep them from doing their job. And she wouldn't either.

Rafe and Cliff followed her onto the porch, their boots clomping hard behind her. She didn't look back but kept on going as fast as her ribs would let her.

"Hold on, would you?" Cliff called, easily catching up to her. "Why are you being so stubborn about this? You're in no shape to be out there on a horse, much less working a branding iron. It's ridiculous."

Oh! She stopped and met his exasperated eyes with a warning glare. "Hold it, bucko, just because you helped me yesterday and then fixed me supper and we had a lovely meal--" and it was a really lovely meal "--it gives you no say in what I do or don't do." This close, Maddie couldn't help noticing how good he looked in the morning sunlight. His scent wrapped around her. His dark brown hair picked up specks of gold in the slanting light. *Focus, Maddie, focus.*

His lip twitched, and then he laughed. *Laughed!*

"Maddie, c'mon. You're too stubborn for your own good. You would hurt yourself just to prove you're going to do things your way. I thought you were smarter than that." He shook his head, spun on his boot heel and strode back across the patio. "Have it your way."

Rafe hadn't said anything as he looked from her to Cliff. After Cliff stalked back inside the house, he shot her a raised, questioning eyebrow. "He's right, you know. There is no reason you need to be out there today. As an owner, there is plenty that you could do here if you had to do something. But honestly, Maddie, take a day off. Rest. Go shopping or get your hair done. Anything. You deserve it."

What was wrong with her hair? Why would he say that?

"Yeah," Chase agreed as he came out onto the patio. "You've been getting a little crazy working ever since C.C. passed on and left us the ranch. He'd tell you straight up to take a rest."

Tears sprang to her eyes thinking about C.C. He would have demanded that she take time off, and she knew it. Feeling foolish suddenly and not liking that at all, she blinked the tears away. Crying would not solve anything. It never had.

"I need to check on my horse." They had no right trying to make her feel bad. Taking a swig of her coffee, she fought through the pain that throbbed throughout her torso with each step she took. She didn't let herself think about how bad it was going to feel when she climbed into the saddle.

They were only trying to help you.

Inside the barn stall, she spoke softly to her gelding when he stuck his head over the top rail. "Hey, buddy," she said, feeling a little tension ease from her as she placed her forehead against his. "What am I doing?" As if he could help her.

She *was* being overly stubborn. She knew it but couldn't seem to stop herself. What was it about Cliff that had her so uptight?

Setting her coffee mug on the bench beside the stall, she went to grab her saddle. As she reached to lift it from its rack, splinters of pain shot through her. Crying out, tears flooding her eyes, she dropped the saddle on the concrete floor. Staring down at it she fought not to cry.

Was she being too stubborn?

* * *

Cliff entered the barn right as Maddie cried out and the saddle thudded to the concrete. Her shoulders slumped and the fight went out of her in a rush.

It hit him hard. She rubbed her forehead, and her eyes closed, probably because she was fighting back the need to cry. His heart cinched tight.

He liked her spunk. Her fire.

Liked that she stood her ground.

But this was unreasonable. What was going on in that pretty head of hers?

"Okay, that does it." He stalked across the fifteen feet to her. "You might be used to getting away with mistreating yourself today, but not when I see how bad you're hurting."

That protective instinct he'd felt from the first moment he'd watched her slam into that pipe fence kicked into overdrive when he saw tears shimmering in her green eyes.

She quickly wiped them away with the back of her hands.

"I'm concerned about you, Maddie. Everyone is."

"I know." She sniffed and wrapped one arm protectively across her ribs. He knew from experience that the pressure helped the pain a little. She opened her mouth to say something more, then shook her head and looked away.

He wanted to pull her close, comfort her, but he sensed she'd push him away.

He hadn't held a woman in months. Hadn't even been tempted as he'd struggled, running on empty. It was a blow when a man realized the dreams he'd been chasing weren't enough. And that was before he learned his dad was dead and the unexpected emotional toll that kicked him with.

What emotions drove this stubborn, kill-herself-with-work need in Maddie?

"Want to talk about it? About why you're doing this to yourself?"

She sniffed and looked away. He waited, giving her

time to get a grip on her emotions, sensing she didn't let people see her cry. Why he knew that he wasn't sure, but he felt like he'd known her for longer than just two days.

"You and I both know as much as I want do, I'm not going to make it onto that horse." A resigned sigh escaped her.

"Yeah, we know that. My question is why are you even trying when there is no reason you need to push yourself like this? I asked the fellas, and they said they have no idea. But that you've been pushing extra hard since your boss died. Since he named you a partner. Why are you doing that, Maddie?"

* * *

Cliff's earnest question tugged at Maddie. "Because there is so much to be done," she blurted out, as if she'd known Cliff all of her life and shared things with him all the time. She didn't share things with anyone. Didn't let people get close. Those walls of disappointment and loss she'd experienced too many times growing up had taught her to keep her emotions close and people on the outside.

She let those she called friends in only so far before the barriers slammed firmly into place. So what was different about Cliff? Other than he'd infuriated her half the time she'd known him.

And rescued her. And made her supper.

And now he's looking at you as if he genuinely cares.

"The way I see it, as big as this ranch is, I'm sure

there's been a lot to do from the day you first hired on. What's driving you now? Is it because you're an owner?"

She looked away, the truth eating at her. The strain of believing she shouldn't be an owner. That she hadn't done enough to deserve the honor. "In a way," she admitted. "Before I was employed by C.C. as a hired hand. I gave a hundred percent to my job, but I didn't have to worry about whether the bills got paid or the ranch grew stronger. I could go to my little apartment at night with no worries."

His shoulders relaxed, and his expression mellowed into understanding. "That makes sense. A *lot* of sense. Especially for a nomad like me who doesn't own anything other than my truck and riding gear. And a few bulls."

Relief eased some of the tension gripping her. "Exactly. It's not like I hadn't planned on settling down eventually. Like you're about to do. I had planned on it too, and soon. You know, buy a small place and make a payment—" She stopped herself from saying more. She certainly wasn't going to blurt out that she had planned to work on letting down the walls around herself in the hopes of finding a soulmate.

"Maddie, Rafe and I talked late into the night, and one of the things we talked about was the ranch. He said y'all are a great team. He said Chase has been doing the books for several years, and that the rest of y'all have different strengths that work well to keep this ranch going strong."

How could she make him understand? "If we each do our part. I'm the weak link." *What are you doing? Why do you want him to understand?*

He laughed. "Yeah, right. No one believes that. Not even me, and I've only known you for two days."

She bit her lip as he suddenly seemed to look even closer into her thoughts. She felt exposed in a way she'd never felt before. As if he could actually see her. Who she really was.

It wasn't realistic. He'd only just met her. But still...

"There's more to this," he said knowingly.

He cupped her jaw gently, surprising her with his touch as much as with what he'd said. She couldn't breathe, and she hadn't been hit by a gate this time.

"I'm not going to press, but if you want to tell me, I'm here and would like to help if you'll let me." His thumb brushed along her jaw.

Longing ached in Maddie's heart, startling her with the intensity of it. She realized that she was staring into Cliff's eyes like a schoolgirl anticipating her first kiss.

She swallowed hard, shaken by the emotions this man had awakened in her.

It didn't make sense. It was too fast.

But right now, she didn't care, because Cliff Masterson had just put a crack in the barrier around her emotions that she'd been trying to figure out how to break open for some time now. And he'd done it with no help from her.

She'd only known him two days. And while that should have scared her silly, it was what captivated her the most.

CHAPTER SIX

Cliff told himself to back off. He had never wanted to kiss a woman as badly or as completely as he wanted to kiss Maddie Rose. Impulsive as he tended to be, he pulled back. This was not the time to let himself have free rein. Maddie was vulnerable, and he knew it. There was something going on inside that beautiful head of hers and maybe even her heart that he didn't want to harm.

She was far more fragile than anyone realized. She had strength and a lot of it, but he'd glimpsed more. Giving in to the need momentarily, he traced her jaw once more with his thumb, then took a step back. Electricity hummed in the air between them.

He gave a shaky chuckle. "You're a stunning, strong woman Maddie. You are far from a weak link. But your body needs a break today. Probably tomorrow, too."

Looking almost as dazed as he felt, she frowned. "I'm not going to lie around and eat cupcakes all day though. I'll go bonkers."

He threw back his head and laughed. "I bet you would. Tell you what. Come help me look at property. I'll drive easy, and if your ribs get to hurting too much, then I'll bring you home to lie down and eat cupcakes."

A little laugh huffed from her. She hesitated, nibbling her lip like he'd seen her do so many times. He almost groaned, thinking about kissing her again. If she rode along, it might make for a rough day now that his thoughts of kissing her had super-glued themselves to his brain.

"I could use your knowledge of the area," he said. When she remained conflicted, he used what he hoped was his ace in the hole. "*And* you do owe me for saving you yesterday."

Her shoulders sagged. "You're right. I owe you."

He felt a stab of disappointment that he'd had to toss out that she owed him in order for her to agree. She didn't owe him anything.

"Great." The important part was that she wouldn't be hurting herself trying to brand cattle or getting into any other trouble she might find when she got bored sitting around. "I really appreciate it."

"It's the least that I can do after what you did for me." She sighed and stared at her dejected saddle sitting on its side. "Could you put my poor mistreated saddle back on that rack for me, please?"

"My pleasure." He winked at her, excitement flashing through him thinking about spending the day with her. "This is going to be a great day."

To his surprise she laughed, or started to, then grabbed her ribs and groaned. Laughter might be the best medicine for most things, but not bruised or busted ribs.

"Ow," she croaked, but her gaze looked bright. Things were looking up.

* * *

Was she really doing this? Maddie wondered again as she walked beside Cliff toward Hailey Bell Sutton's real estate office. Of course, that wasn't what had her feeling like she'd jumped off a cliff. It was that she was actually going to *try* and crack the shell around her emotions. Cliff had gotten past a boundary no one else ever had. Could she let him in further?

They'd called ahead to make sure Hailey was at the office. These days it was uncertain, since Hailey was almost nine months pregnant and due any day. She was in and had questioned Cliff over the phone and promised to have property suggestions ready when they arrived at her office on Main Street.

Hailey was a gorgeous blonde and one of the nicest people in town. And that was saying a lot, because Mule Hollow was loaded with a full deck of good people. She waved them in as soon as she spotted them through the window.

"Hey, Maddie, y'all come in and have a seat. And please excuse me for not standing up." She rubbed her huge tummy and smiled widely. "Doctor's orders, and he has my husband, Will, lined up as my bouncer should I not comply. I can come to work, but I have to sit. If I do more than waddle to the bathroom after I get here, then I can't come to work anymore." She smiled, looking extremely happy, then held her hand out to Cliff.

"And you must be Cliff? It is so nice to meet you. And exciting that you're going to settle here." They shook hands, and then she waved them to the chairs across from her. "You'll love it, and from a real estate perspective, there's a lot to choose from hidden across the county. And at pretty fair prices."

When they were seated, she handed him a stack of photos and pages of property descriptions.

"Thanks," Cliff said, his smile had widened as the words had rolled from Hailey at a fast clip. He thumbed through the pages quickly. "These look great."

"I hope there's something in there you'll like." She looked from him to Maddie with interest. "I'm glad you're going with him, since you're familiar with the area. I'll feel less like I'm abandoning him with you along."

"I'm glad to do it," Maddie said, still in shock that she was contemplating pushing the feelings Cliff stirred in her.

She and Hailey chatted about the baby while Cliff looked more closely at the pages. Maddie couldn't help but be a little envious of Hailey. She really wanted a baby. Not that she ever talked about it to anyone. If she talked about it, then she'd have to explain to her friends why she was afraid she'd never have children of her own. Truth was, when a person was as afraid as she was of showing her heart to someone, well, it made falling in love pretty hard. And if she wasn't falling in love, there wasn't a possibility of her having a baby. It was complicated.

When Cliff finished choosing the properties he wanted to see, there were a total of six listings in his hand. None of them had an owner on the premises, so they didn't have to set up any appointments, which made viewing easy.

"Hopefully, I'll still be around by the time you find something," Hailey said before they left. "But if I'm not, my friend Sugar Rae will step in. She was my assistant for several years and is going to fill in part time, finishing up any deals that I leave dangling. So you don't have to worry about that."

"I wasn't worried." Cliff shook her hand again. "You take care of yourself and don't worry about us. We'll be fine."

Easy for him to say, Maddie thought. If he could only see into the mass confusion inside her mind! If he could, then he'd know she had absolutely no idea whether she was going to be fine or not.

Within minutes they were heading out of town. Maddie told herself to relax and enjoy the day and the— she searched for the right word for what she was doing— *possibilities*. She was exploring possibilities.

The thought made her smile inside.

What was the worst thing that could happen? That by the end of the day her attraction to him wasn't strong enough to take a risk for what she wanted?

Or was it that at the end of the day she'd realize his interest wasn't strong enough to break completely through her emotional shields?

Either of those scenarios would put her right back where she'd been before he'd shown up yesterday.

She could handle that. She could.

At least she'd be able to say she put herself out there.

She'd taken a risk.

She was calm by the time they reached the first property. It was a nice place. Not far from Horizon Ranch, it had stock pens that sat off from the house, and its location appealed to Cliff.

It was a pretty morning, with the sun flirting with them through fluffy clouds as they pulled to a halt near the barn and the cattle pens.

"Nope," he said after a quick scan of the area. "This isn't it."

She laughed, shocked by his reaction. "But you didn't even get out of the truck."

"I didn't need to. What's the next one?"

He'd lined them up in the order that he wanted to see them, so she pulled the next one off the list. "Here it is. Are you sure you even want to bother driving out there?"

His eyes crinkled at the edges. "Yes, I want to drive out there. This one had points against it coming in. It's the smallest on the list, with less than a two hundred acres, which is a little small for what I need. And the pens need a lot of work, and they're too close to the house."

"I see what you're saying." She gave him directions to the next place. "At this rate we'll be home by noon," she joked…and seriously hoped not.

He talked about what he was looking for as they drove to the next listing. She liked listening to the cadence in his voice and deep timbre of it. She'd been too upset and aggravated to enjoy anything the day before when they'd been in the truck together. She'd been too busy thinking about strangling him.

"You said you're going to raise rodeo stock? Right?" she asked.

"I'm going to raise bulls. The stock I raise will be strictly for my own cattle business, and it won't be a large herd, so this acreage would work."

He was standing with his hands on his hips taking in the house, pens and surrounding acreage of the second listing. He looked impossibly perfect in that moment. Impossibly appealing. She pushed the negative thought away and struggled to be positive.

"Are you giving up riding them?" She held her breath, knowing if he said yes that would mean he wouldn't be an absentee owner.

"I'm thinking about it." His eyes met hers and held before he headed across the yard to the house, a brick home with a large porch overlooking the pastures. There were some huge old oak trees shading the yard, and though it wasn't as spectacular as the patio of the ranch house C.C. had built, it was homey and appealing.

The flare of attraction burned strong and bold as she

followed him. And it had only grown stronger as the morning had progressed.

Hailey had warned them that the house had sat vacant for many years and was in need of repair. While Cliff unlocked the door, she peeked in the windows. "Hailey wasn't kidding. The place is crying out for help."

She had to pass close to Cliff as she walked through the doorway. Her pulse hummed with his nearness, and she almost leaned in and inhaled.

Soap and aftershave had never smelled so good.

There was some kind of chemistry bubbling between she and Cliff, chemistry she'd never, *ever* experienced before. Rafe, Ty, Chase and Dalton were amazing, hunky, handsome cowboys. When they spruced up for one of their dates, they smelled good too. But she'd never had the urge to tackle one of them!

Okay. Now her imagination was getting out of hand.

Time to put some space between her and this cowboy. Moving quickly, she headed to the far side of the room to study the fireplace and then the kitchen, as if her life depended on it.

She forced her mind to the task of evaluating the property, *not* Cliff. The place had been vacant for over ten years, since the area's oil boom had dried up and folks had been forced to move away for jobs. It was apparent that it had once been a nice place, but time and neglect had taken their toll.

Not a problem Cliff had. He was perfect.

"I don't know."

She jumped at Cliff's voice and focused. He was looking about skeptically.

"A buyer might be better off starting from scratch and building."

Maddie cringed when a rodent scurried down the hall and disappeared into a bedroom. "You might be right." She hadn't been able to get any good feelings going about the place. Of course that could very likely be because all of her feelings were preoccupied with Cliff. And now the rodent.

"Then let's move on to the next place." He shot her a smile. "We have all day. I'm not feeling excited about the house. And I can see in your eyes that you aren't either."

Maddie hoped that was all he could see in her eyes. "Right. We have a lot of places to choose from." She was almost to the door when she realized that she'd said "we," as if it mattered if she liked the place.

Back off now. You'll only be hurt if you invest any more of yourself. And you are acting way too unlike yourself, sister.

Maddie knew she should listen to the voice of warning, but she'd promised herself that she would push herself. And that was exactly what she planned to do.

Of course she wasn't getting crazy or anything, and that meant not being reckless. There was no "we" in this equation. She was just a gal trying to get to know a guy.

There was nothing wrong with that. Nothing.

It was natural. Holing up with herself and her stinkin' fear of letting someone close—that was the thing that was wrong.

CHAPTER SEVEN

The scent of home cooking and the rowdy tones of Toby Keith playing on the jukebox greeted them as Maddie and Cliff slid into a booth at Sam's Diner. The hub of the town, the rustic diner was where Mule Hollow folks congregated all through the day to eat and catch up on the latest goings on. Cliff liked the place.

"Hi, Sam," Maddie called across the room to the tiny man behind the counter.

Sam was short and small like a jockey, with a weatherworn face and intelligent eyes. Cliff had been in the diner several times when his shoulder had been hurt. Had even played some checkers with App and Stanley, a couple of retired ranchers who had checker battles every morning over coffee and sunflower seeds.

"Hey, Cliff. Heard you were in town," Sam said, coming their way.

Sam had a legendary fierce grip, and Cliff braced for it as Sam clamped down hard.

"I hear you're looking for land around here. You getting out of the PBR?" Sam asked.

The Professional Bull Riders circuit had been Cliff's world for years. *Was it now?* He had an event coming up in about two weeks. He hadn't decided what he was going to do about it.

Cliff was aware of Maddie watching him. He grinned at Sam. "News travels fast around here."

"Small town. You gotta be quick to get somethin' by all of them well-meaning busybodies. Particularly App and Stanley." Sam chuckled, his entire face crinkling with laughter. "My wife, sweet as she is, included. They were all in here talkin' about you two around breakfast. One of them saw y'all over at Hailey Bell this mornin' together. Stirred up quite a dither."

Maddie's eyes widened. "I was helping Cliff."

"That's reasonable. So are you done riding bulls professionally?" Sam asked again.

"No. Taking a break is all. I'm making some changes." Cliff knew he was going to come across this question a lot, but he wasn't ready to talk about it. He was still trying to understand why things had been different since learning his dad was dead. He hadn't seen his dad in six years. And it had only been that one time since the day he'd left home. He pushed the thoughts away. Now was not the time to contemplate that part of his life.

"The PBR has been good to me, and I have some commitments. But I figure it's time to start looking past bull riding to raising them."

"Smart. We've got a few folks around here who do that."

More folks came in, so Sam took their orders of burgers, then headed off in the direction of the kitchen.

"Where's App and Stanley?" Cliff asked, glancing over at the table by the window where the two old checker players were usually hunched over their game.

"They start the day early and are usually back home before lunch." She chuckled. "You have to be early to catch them. Breakfast till brunch is their time."

"I forgot. I'll have to swing by one morning and say hello. I met them when I was here before. Really enjoyed my visit."

Maddie smiled. "It's a great town."

"Yeah, I haven't been by to see Rafe as often as I should."

"You've been busy, had commitments."

"Yeah, I did. But..." He rested his elbows on the table and cupped his hands as he glanced around. He knew it was more than that. He'd been running. He'd only just realized that was what he'd been doing. "Rafe is my only family. It will be nice to see him more."

Something shadowed in her eyes, and he wondered what she was thinking as she studied him. "It's nice to have family. You're right, you shouldn't take it lightly or for granted."

"What about your family, Maddie? Where do they live?" He'd realized that she talked less about her past than he did. And he was curious. He knew that just because someone didn't talk about their past it didn't mean that they'd lived with an abusive drunk like he and Rafe had. Some people didn't talk about their past because they were private people.

Not because thinking of the past made them angry.

"I—" she hesitated, as if weighing what she wanted to say. "I was raised in foster care. My parents gave me up when I was a baby."

Sam brought their tea and burgers, and Cliff hardly even noticed. "I'm sorry." He felt like an oaf because he could see in Maddie's eyes, those expressive eyes, that damage had been done. He knew there was an abundance of good caring folks out there who opened up their homes for hurting and abandoned kids. He prayed Maddie's had been good. He also knew there were plenty of them who housed as many as allowed for the steady source of income it provided them. "You had good people, right?"

"They were fine." She took a bite of her burger. "Sam makes the best burgers."

It didn't take a kindergartner to recognize her evasion.

He was about to ask for more when a group of young wranglers entered the diner and took the table across from them.

"Hey, man! That's Cliff Masterson," one of them declared.

"Wow, I watched you win the Bull Riding Championship down in Houston two years ago," another one added.

Within seconds Cliff was the one back in the hot seat, bombarded with questions about bulls and competition. Before he knew it, lunch was over, and they were heading outside an hour later.

"That was nice of you to agree to give them

pointers," Maddie said as he took her elbow to help her step up on the running board and then into the seat.

"I had some help when I started out. I recognize the fresh, hungry look on their faces. Gotta give back sometimes."

She studied him "You might irritate the fire out of me being bossy and all, but you're a nice guy." A smile hovered on her lips.

He leaned over her to buckle the seatbelt for her because he knew she would have trouble, holding her gaze as he did it. Her sweet scent and that smile had been driving him crazy all day. "You're rubbing off on me."

She laughed. "Did you forget how mad I got yesterday?"

"You're a woman with some fire to her. That doesn't mean you're not sweet."

She was, and he knew it. Instinctively he knew much of her spunk had probably come from defensiveness because of her background. He understood that his past had shaped him too.

They stared at each other. She swallowed hard and held his gaze. Before he could stop himself, he leaned in and kissed her. And just like when he climbed on the back of a bull, he realized this could go one of two ways.

It could go good or it could go bad.

And it would only take eight seconds or less to know.

* * *

Maddie was so startled when Cliff dipped his head and

covered her lips with his that she froze, her mind reeling, her senses exploding as his warm breath mingled with hers. Everything blurred, her eyes drifted closed, and she found herself responding to his touch, to the gentleness of the kiss. The tenderness of his fingertips lightly tracing her jawline, then cupping her head, drawing her closer as he deepened the kiss.

Maddie's heart thundered in her chest. She was lost in the feel of his firm lips moving over hers.

When he pulled back, his breathing ragged, his eyes probing he looked as dazed as she was.

What had just happened?

"I'm sorry," he said, and an instant later he closed the door and headed around the truck.

Maddie's heart hammered. She struggled to catch her breath as she gripped the door handle and let the world slowly stop spinning.

Let it gradually come back into focus.

Only then did she remember that it was right past lunchtime, and Cliff had just planted a smokin' hot kiss on her—*right smack in the middle of Main Street.*

Right where anyone who was looking would see.

Glancing around she groaned, because standing on the sidewalk two doors down stood Esther Mae Wilcox, Norma Sue Jenkins and Sam's wife, Adela Ledbetter Green.

Better known as the Match Makin' Posse of Mule Hollow.

CHAPTER EIGHT

As he climbed into the truck, Cliff's insides were all jangled up. He cranked the key, shifted to reverse and, in a daze, backed out of the parking lot.

What had he been thinking?

He'd hauled off and let his impulsive nature take hold of him, kissing Maddie right out of the blue like that.

Right there in front of Sam's Diner for the entire world to see.

The realization of what he'd done got lost in the euphoria of the kiss though. Man, had that been something.

He glanced over at Maddie, hoping she wasn't as mad as he feared she might be. Her blistering gaze instantly shot that hope to pieces.

"What's wrong?" The truck was stopped, and he hesitated, his hand on the shift ready to ram it into drive. He hadn't expected her to be *that* mad.

"What's wrong? That is." She lifted a hand in a

hesitant wave.

His gazed followed hers.

He'd only been here two weeks when he'd visited Rafe, but he knew exactly who the ladies were waving at them from the sidewalk.

He groaned. Waved. And hit the gas.

* * *

Maddie woke before dawn and headed out to the barn. She was moving a little better and glad of it. It took a lot of struggling, but she got her horse saddled.

The kiss, despite everything, remained on Maddie's mind all afternoon and through the night. She'd overreacted when she'd realized the matchmakers had witnessed the kiss.

Yes, they may have ideas now—okay, there was no doubt that when three known matchmakers witnessed a kiss in broad daylight on the main drag of town—they were going to get ideas.

All *kinds* of ideas and all of them were going to end with a matchmaking plan. Her sleepless night couldn't change that.

There was nothing to be done about it.

But that kiss. That amazing, gentle kiss that had whispered to the deepest dark corners of her wounded heart, where dreams and fear clung together...

She'd lost her good sense yesterday.

These feelings he'd initiated inside of her could get

out of hand. Spending time with him in large doses could be dangerous to her heart.

Maddie tightened her horse's cinch and girded up her emotions at the same time, and then headed to the house. Everyone would be in the kitchen by now.

She prepared herself for their protest, but as far as she was concerned, she was working today. And that was final.

Cliff, his smile wide and welcoming, was the first handsome face her wretched gaze sought out. Oh, dear goodness, but the man took her breath away.

How could anyone look so good leaning against the counter drinking a glass of orange juice?

But with lean, corded muscles honed from years of bull riding, his dark hair curling at his collar and his blue eyes gleaming like stained glass shot through with sunbeams, he could have sold orange juice by the case. Her mouth went dry.

He was the epitome of every Prince Charming she'd ever dreamed of as a lonely young girl growing up.

No doubt about it, it was time for her to put some distance between her and Cliff.

"You were outside early. How are you feeling this morning?" he asked.

"Fine," she said, then, unable to lie, added, "Sore, but better."

Rafe handed her a mug of coffee. "Second day is always the worst. You'd better take it easy again today."

"Thanks, but I've already saddled my horse. I'm going

today."

"Told y'all. I win." Chase gave a triumphant laugh.

"Win what?" She looked about the room.

"Chase said you'd be going this morning." Dalton grinned.

Maddie wasn't sure how to take this information. "And y'all didn't think I would be."

"Now, don't go getting all riled up. We figured you'd be hurting worse today than yesterday."

Ty grabbed a pan of biscuits from the oven. "You need to heal up."

"You don't have to help on our account. You need to take care of yourself." Dalton flipped bacon in a pan.

Cliff's husky chuckle touched her from across the room and made her feel his kiss again. Her stomach clenched, and she shot him a glare, not at all happy with the way every cell in her body was straining toward him.

"I'm coming, so end of story," she snapped, then headed back outside. "Hurry your breakfast, boys. Daylight's burnin'."

No sooner had she sat down on the patio chair to wait on the fellas to finish than Cliff followed her outside. "Don't even try to talk me out of this," she warned, shoring up her defenses against letting herself fall for him.

He pulled out a chair and sat down. "I figured this was what you'd do. Are you still mad about the kiss?"

Yes. The dull ache of her ribs was a reminder of how much more a broken heart could hurt. "This is not a good idea, Cliff."

His jaw tensed, and he rubbed the back of his neck. "I shouldn't have kissed you. Not so soon and not like that where it could cause you trouble. That's the last thing I'd want to do."

She couldn't look at him.

"Make sure you've wrapped your ribs good. You have wrapped them?" he asked gently.

Completely surprised that he wasn't trying to tell her she didn't need to go, she stared at him. "Yes, I have."

He was looking out for her. Just like yesterday but in a completely different way. *How was she supposed to handle that?*

"I figured you'd wrapped them, but I wanted you to know I cared."

Her pulse skipped a beat at the sincerity in his voice. She needed that distance she'd decided on. She stood too quickly, and her ribs let her know it. But she had to put some space between them. And she had to do it now.

The guys came out of the house at that moment, and she wanted to hug them. Their timing was so perfect. No one had ever put this much effort into flustering her!

"Let's load up," Chase said, winking at Maddie.

"Y'all don't work her too hard," Cliff warned.

Maddie headed toward the trucks that would pull the trailers of horses and carry them all out to the part of the ranch they would work today. "They don't determine how hard I work," she tossed over her shoulder, feeling churlish. "I do. I'll do what I want out there." That said, she climbed into the cab of the truck and slammed the door.

She was startled to see him climb into one of the other trucks. "He's going with us?" she asked Chase when he got behind the wheel.

"Yup. He always helps us some when he comes down. He loves working cattle."

She bit back a groan. Well, if he thought he was going to be her nursemaid today, he was wrong.

She had been doing fine before he came along. She'd made it just fine without someone following her and bossing her around.

Worrying about her.

Doing nice things for her.

She didn't need any of that. She didn't.

* * *

"She'll slow down when she needs to, Cliff," Rafe warned from the saddle of his horse. "You have to give a woman like Maddie her space. If you're thinking you like her, like I'm thinking you do, then you'd better lay low and get to know the real Maddie Rose. She doesn't take to coddling too well."

Cliff's movements were jerky as he pulled his rope, recoiling it after they finished with the calf he'd dragged over to be branded. He'd been roping and dragging calves to the fire all morning while Maddie administered the meds and shots. Chase branded them, and Ty tagged them. At the rate they were going, they'd be finished by early afternoon. It felt good to be cowboy'n, and he'd been glad Rafe had invited him along. Though honestly, he'd come because he wanted to be near Maddie.

He had to admit that Maddie wasn't slowing them down. The constant up and down had to be killing her ribs, but he could see the truth in his brother's words. He was going to have to give her room. After all, she'd only known him three days.

His downfall had always been that when he saw something he wanted, he went after it with gusto. His determination had always been his strong suit. But he did tend to steamroll his way into things. Apparently, that wasn't the way to win Maddie's favor.

By noon, they were all filthy, and the sun had them all beat down a bit. Maddie was moving more slowly, though she wasn't going to admit it. But why did she think she had to prove anything with her friends? Didn't she know that it was okay to slow down and show a little vulnerability?

Of course, she was a woman in a male dominated world.

By one o'clock they had the last calf branded, tagged and vaccinated. Maddie pulled off her gloves and wiped the sweat out of her eyes as they gathered around the water cooler.

Cliff filled up a cup and handed it to her. Their fingers brushed, and that tsunami of awareness crashed through him. "Great job, today."

"Thanks," she said, her voice gritty from all the dusty air that hovered about them. She downed water in three gulps. Despite her sun-kissed skin, there was a paleness to her.

He pulled his gaze away from her, then moved over so others could get to the cooler. It was taking every ounce of determination he had not to ask Maddie how she felt.

What he wanted to do was scoop her into his arms and make her take it easy and rest her ribs. He wanted to take care of her.

"You still holding out okay?" Rafe asked her.

"Doing fine." She shot him a smile—*a smile!*

Cliff holstered his irritation. If he'd asked her that, she wouldn't have sent that dazzling smile his way.

"I've got business in town. I'll see y'all later," he practically growled. He stalked across to his truck and hauled out of there like an idiot. Jealousy had never been a problem of his. Today, he was as green as it got. Frustration played a part in it. He was about as frustrated as a man could be.

He'd never had these kinds of reactions to a woman before.

He was in new territory. Maddie had turned his world upside down.

CHAPTER NINE

Maddie figured she'd made her point. Two days straight she'd helped work cattle like the rest of her partners. She'd worked hard, and her body ached, but there were good signs that tomorrow would be better.

The first day when Cliff had come along, she'd expected him to scowl and tell her to take it easy. Instead he'd backed off, and it had been Rafe and the gang who'd watched her like hawks. If she didn't know any better—and she did—they were hoping Cliff would open his mouth and she'd explode. *The mud-grubbers.* But he hadn't. Oh, he wasn't happy, and every time their gazes had met, she knew it. But he kept his opinion to himself.

Today he hadn't come along, choosing instead to look at more properties. He'd seemed a little disgruntled at breakfast and headed off soon after she'd walked into the kitchen.

As odd as it was, she'd missed sparring with him today. It was actually fun. Did that make her weird?

She had obviously been kicked in the head by Buford.

Cliff remained on her mind Friday after work. She'd cleaned up and headed to town for a meeting about the festival coming up in a week. With all the Buford and Cliff shenanigans, she'd almost forgotten she'd gotten roped into helping them. Once she'd remembered her commitment, she'd tried not to stress about it. She was doing pretty good too, considering the meeting involved the matchmakers. She was anticipating a lot of questions.

Three weeks ago, Norma Sue had snookered her by saying since Maddie was now a landowner, it would be good for her to get involved helping the town's economy. Maddie wasn't so sure she believed the matchmaker's reason, especially since she hadn't gone to the guys with the same request. But she *was* a landowner now. And the fellas had agreed to help her with the riding lesson pen she'd chosen to be involved with, so that was good.

"Yoo-hoo, Maddie, over here!" Esther Mae called, her bright red hair standing out like a beacon the moment Maddie walked into Sam's.

"Where is everyone?" she asked, assuming the other ladies who helped run the festivals would be here. Lacy, the local hairstylist, was a huge help and usually in on the meetings. There were several others too, but the older ladies and Lacy were the hub of the group.

Norman Sue shook her head. "Lacy's tied up trying to rescue Maureen Simpson from her self-inflicted color disaster. Poor woman has messed herself up but good."

Esther May harrumphed. "It's terrible. Looks like she dipped her head in a can of black tar. Every time she gets bored, she does something different to her hair, and poor Lacy has to fix the problem."

"Some people are restless that way," Adela said.

Maddie had never heard the gentle lady utter a bad word about anyone.

"True." Norma Sue grinned wide, her plump cheeks shiny. "If Esther Mae had that notion, there is no telling *what* her hair would look like."

Esther Mae looked appalled. "Ha! I have other things that keep my attention. For one, Maddie and her cowboy. Tell us about that good-lookin' hunk you were kissing the other day."

Maddie felt a headache coming on. She'd known this was coming.

Adela leaned toward her and squeezed her arm with her delicate hand. "We'd heard Rafe's twin brother was back in town. Such a nice looking young man."

"Cliff. Yes, he is." It was true. He was nice. Maddening and bossy at times, but a nice guy. She thought about the way her pulse had skittered as she'd sneaked a peek at him while he was riding his horse and roping calves. Hunk described him perfectly. She realized all three ladies were watching her with big grins.

"I was showing him property," she added quickly. It was a lame, evasive attempt. "I was only helping him out."

"Looked like he needed a lot of help." Norma Sue

chuckled, her eyes twinkling.

Maddie had stepped right into that one.

Esther Mae tapped her packet of diet sweetener on the table top like a gavel. "Honey, there is nothing wrong with kissing a man. You need to be doing more of that. We've been worried about you. Isn't that right, Norma Sue?"

"Absolutely." Her friend jumped in with both feet. "Kissing is great. Don't think because we're older than you that we don't enjoy our fair share. That Roy Don still turns my head every time he ambles into a room. But if you're always working like you are, then you're never gonna find time to meet a man to smooch with."

Maddie almost choked on her water.

Adela bobbed her dewy, white-haired head in agreement. "And that is exactly why we were so delighted to see you snuggled up to him on Tuesday."

"You need to get out more," Esther Mae said. "It's healthy, and, honey, you're supposed to have some fun. Go to the movies, out to eat. To a festival, which we happen to have a lot of."

Norma Sue was grinning widely again. "That's right. Festivals give our cowboys and cowgirls like you a chance to kick up your boots every once in a while."

"Okay. I'm helping at the festival." Maddie stared at the matchmakers, a little stupefied by their logic. She'd been afraid of this, but it wasn't so bad.

And what had Cliff really done?

Made her wake up?

Made her want to finally confront her fear of abandonment?

As if it had been planned beforehand, Maddie heard a familiar, delicious laugh and shot a startled glance over her shoulder. Sure enough, there was Cliff walking into the diner with the group of cowboys he'd promised to give bull riding tips to. His gaze locked onto hers like she was the only person in the crowded diner.

His laughter stalled and tension cracked between them like a bull whip. His eyes warmed, a slow smile tickled Maddie's insides as if he'd just traced the curve of her cheek with his fingertips. Or teased her lips with a brush of his lips on hers.

Oh, goodness.

Esther Mae's sigh from across the table made Maddie jump and snap to.

She had a romantic movie moment. A boy-meets-girl-sigh-worthy moment that Maddie had never experienced before, not personally. She'd watched many a chick-flick over the years and experienced moments like that.

But this was a first.

"Yoo-hoo, Cliff. Over here," Esther Mae called.

Maddie's jaw dropped, and it was crawl under the table time.

Cliff parted from his friends and came their way. His long legs had him to the table in three strides.

His smile continued to dazzle as he held out his hand to each of the ladies. "It's been a long time, ladies. Y'all look like you're doing well and having a good time."

"Oh, *we are*," Esther Mae cooed. "We were actually discussing our Maddie here."

Maddie went on full alert.

Norma Sue pushed back her white Stetson. "We've been thinking that our Maddie should get out more. You know, date more, and we're just thrilled to pieces about the two of you."

Oh, no. Maddie had relaxed. Forgotten she'd let the ladies see her thoughts. They were good at reading signs of attraction. She almost rubbed the tension that had formed smack in the middle of her eyes but caught herself before doing it. Instead she willed her expression to relax as Cliff's amused gaze slid to hers.

"I can't imagine Maddie not having dates lined up from here to the next county," he said, sounding like he meant what he said.

Norma Sue frowned. "Oh, she could, but she works all the time. We're trying to pull her out of the pasture more."

"That's right," Esther Mae interrupted in a rush. "There's more to life than riding a horse and roping a bunch of cows."

Surely this wasn't happening.

"I couldn't agree more." Cliff grinned, and Maddie scowled nervously at him. He knew exactly what he was doing adding fuel to the meddlesome posse's bonfire. They were eating it up.

"Matter of fact," he said, milking the whole ordeal for all it was worth. "I heard the theater on the outskirts of town is great, and I was going to see if Maddie would go with me this weekend. Maybe y'all could help a cowboy out and put in a good word for me."

If she hadn't been so mad at him, she would have laughed. He was really cute and having such a fun time teasing her. And that was what he was doing, she knew it. But still, *pleaseLouise*, he was about to make her life hard.

The problem was that he had no idea who he was dealing with, while the innocent looking posse knew *exactly* what they were doing.

At least she thought they did. Their matchmaking resume had blossomed into the high double digits in the last few years.

That lit their eyes up, and if Cliff had been sitting down, Maddie would have kicked him under the table for encouraging them!

"That's perfect, Maddie," Adela encouraged. "You should do that."

"But—"

"Maddie," Esther Mae joined in. "It's not healthy the way you work all the time."

"I like working," Maddie argued. "And no one says anything about it when a man works like that. Norma Sue, you're a ranch woman. You know what it's like." It was true. Norma Sue loved her work. The woman wore overalls or jeans all the time with boots and her white Stetson.

"She's got you on that, Norma," Esther Mae agreed.

"Hold on. I love ranch work, sure do. But when I met my Roy Don, that man made my heart start thinking of other things. Believe me, I was more than ready to get out of the sun and make a life with that cowboy." She grinned. "Like we told you a few minutes ago, there is a *lot* more to life than cattle. Some really good stuff. Like that kissin' you and this good lookin' hunk of cowboy were doing the other day."

Maddie rubbed her suddenly clammy hands on her thighs as heat suffused her cheeks and thoughts of that kiss she'd shared with Cliff came to mind. No matter how much she tried not to think about it, she wouldn't mind doing it again. Her gaze flicked to his, and he smiled as if he could read her mind!

Laughter crinkled the edges of his eyes. "Sounds good to me."

Maddie's mind reeled. She didn't remember the matchmakers ever, *ever,* being so blunt and to the point. Did they consider her that desperate? Or that hard to find a match for?

If they only knew how badly she wanted a family. How she struggled with making ranching be enough fulfillment for her because she didn't think anyone could ever love her enough to stick around. Or that she'd let them close enough.

Sadly, she knew that the way the ladies depicted her was exactly how it would be if she didn't make some changes.

Esther Mae patted the edge of her short red hair. "A

woman has to show the fellas she's available. Why, Maddie you've got walls up a mile high, and they need to be torn down. Cliff, don't you think that would be fun?"

Maddie gasped. "Esther Mae!" This was beyond okay.

Cliff's brows dipped.

"Oh, I didn't mean nothing mean about that," Esther Mae said, actually looking sheepish. "I—"

"She gets carried away sometimes." Adela apologized, giving her friend a gentle warning look.

Cliff cocked his head and his eyes thoughtful. "The man who falls for Maddie needs to love her for the woman she is. Maddie here needs a partner with a vision for the same things she wants. I wouldn't change anything about her."

Maddie's stomach tumbled a few times, and her heart followed. Humiliation burned her cheeks as she hated to think what Cliff might be thinking after all of this craziness.

His expression shifted with sincerity. "I'm serious, Maddie. I really would love to take you to the theater. But only if you want to go."

Maddie didn't have to see the other three pairs of eyes to know that they shared her focus on Cliff. Maddie could feel their matchmaking minds speed into overdrive.

Her heart raced out of control at his words, and she didn't know whether to whack him with a menu for helping create this fiasco or thank him for the invitation.

Norma Sue elbowed her. "Say something, Maddie.

He's good."

Maddie stood up. "Fine. I'll go." She looked about the table. "But, so you know, I understand exactly what just happened here. And y'all do not play fair." Zeroed in on the exit, she didn't stop until she was at her truck.

Her life had just turned into a circus.

And she'd accepted a date with Cliff...

CHAPTER TEN

"I have a date with Maddie," Cliff told Rafe a few hours after the incident at the diner.

They had met at one of the neighboring ranch arenas to watch the group of young cowboys ride bulls like he'd promised.

Cliff was still reeling over what had happened in the diner. He wasn't real sure the posse wasn't a few cards short of a full deck. He hadn't appreciated them making Maddie feel bad about herself. Although he didn't think that was what they'd meant to do, he'd seen it in her eyes. Some of the advice they'd offered could do her some good. But still...wow, they'd poured it on strong.

The truth was, he'd walked right into their little setup with his eyes wide open.

Sure he was teasing Maddie and going along with them before it had gotten out of hand. But *only* because he could sense that they really cared about Maddie. They wanted good things for her. Still, they'd gotten a little carried away.

And Adela had completely blindsided him when she'd been the one who suggested the date.

He'd gotten serious when he realized Maddie thought he was having a good time toying with her.

"Really?" Rafe said.

"You don't have a problem with that, do you?"

Rafe had his arms crossed and hanging over the edge of the arena. He cocked his head at Cliff. "None. Just treat her with respect."

"And you actually thought you had to tell me that." Cliff was no saint, but he wasn't some womanizing, love 'em and leave 'em jerk.

"No, that's not it. You need to know Maddie is special."

"I know that."

"I don't know if you do. She doesn't date, and we've all noticed that. She's become like a little sister to us, but we don't pry. She's private, and the fact that she's accepted a date with you is a good thing. I'm thinking you need to know the full score, though. I think she could be hurt real easy. She's not as tough as she wants us all to think."

"I had figured some of that out, but thanks for filling me in," Cliff said.

Rafe turned toward him. "Look, I know we had a crummy background, and I know you've been running around the country trying to outrun it all these years."

He stared at Rafe in disbelief. "How do you know that? I didn't even realize it until I found out Dad was dead." He laughed harsh, bitter. "It doesn't even make sense to me. I love riding bulls. But no matter how hard I tried to settle down, I couldn't do it. The minute I heard the news, it was like some fist inside me unclenched."

"I know."

"How do you know that?"

"You're not the only one who was angry. I was just forced to deal with it before you. When my knee blew out, I couldn't run from the past anymore. C.C. helped me understand it. That man had a way of looking at a people and knowing what they needed."

Cliff stared at his brother. "What did you need?"

"A place to be at peace. A place to belong and feel a sense of accomplishment. Ending up at the ranch grounded me like I'd never had before. Certainly not in our home growing up."

No, their home growing up had been as loud and dysfunctional as it got. "He was a piece of work, wasn't he?" Cliff took a deep breath. Tension had coiled tight when he thought about his father. Now it eased out of him as he exhaled.

"Yeah, and then some." Rafe snorted. "If Mom hadn't gotten sick and died, I guess she'd have stayed with him until the end."

They were silent for a moment, the sadness of that statement a deep gash of pain in each of them.

"I guess love is not always easy to understand." It was all Cliff could come up with. He'd stopped trying to figure out his mother a long time ago. "So why haven't you found me a nice sister-in-law and settled down and given me some nieces and nephews?" he asked, changing the subject.

Rafe's expression shadowed. "Hey, don't rush me, and I won't rush you. Like you said, love's not always easy to understand, and I sure don't have it figured out."

Had Rafe been in love?

"Me, either." Cliff thought of Maddie and the date that couldn't get here soon enough.

"Show's about to start," Rafe said, changing the subject again. "You better get up there. These fellas are expecting you to turn them into champions. So get to work."

Cliff chuckled. "I'll do my best. It might be time to pass the torch."

* * *

Maddie was loading up calf feeding bottles and dealing with the shock of having said yes to a date with Cliff the day before.

Her mind still hadn't wrapped around the events of the diner episode, and she'd tossed and turned with it all night long. Her pillow was probably sore from the workout she'd given it.

"Hey. Good morning."

The sound of Cliff's voice caused her insides to jumble nervously. It was both a dangerous and good feeling at the same time.

When she glanced at him, the air felt alive with electricity.

"Good morning." She closed the tailgate and tried not to seem affected. *Yeah, right.*

"Did you sleep good?"

She cut you've-got-to-be-kidding eyes at him. Getting mad and mortified all over again about the ambush.

"Look, about all of that yesterday. I'm sorry if it embarrassed you or made you uncomfortable."

"It was kind of hard not to be. Don't you think? You heard what they said. For goodness' sake, I didn't realize exactly how pitiful I was until they pointed it out to me." Okay, so she hadn't meant to let those feelings out of the bag. She felt bad enough knowing them herself.

He looked uncomfortable. "I don't think they meant it that way. I really don't."

She sighed and looked away, studying Ty in the distance working with a horse in the early morning light. Finally, she looked back at Cliff. Crossing her arms over ribs that barely hurt any more. "I know. But I hope you know that the posse has declared us their next matchmaking project. You do realize that, right?"

"Yeah, I might have started out with blinders on yesterday but I picked up on that."

Surprisingly that made her lips twitch with the need to smile. "Well, I hope you're prepared."

He hitched a brow, and his lips curved into a smirk. "I ain't scared. Are you?"

"I'm not scared of anything," she blurted, her pulse

pounding at his words.

He sobered. "I believe that for the most part. But everyone's scared of something."

Maddie's hands tightened on her arms. "I'm going to feed a couple of orphaned calves. Would you like to ride along?" The invitation was out before she could stop it or analyze it. Maybe she was trying to prove to him she wasn't scared.

But she was terrified, and she knew it.

* * *

Cliff had jumped on the offer from Maddie like a man diving into the last lifeboat on a sinking ship. The fact that she'd asked him to come along, especially after seeing how miffed she was, meant a lot. He tried not to read too much into it, but he knew he was. With everything he learned about Maddie, he was more and more drawn to her. He wanted to see what she enjoyed. Wanted to get to know the woman who held people at bay.

And he sensed with every yard of pasture they crossed that orphaned calves meant something.

It had rained sometime in the night, and more was threatening as she showed him the barn and feedlot where they kept the orphans and their new "adoptive" mamas, as she called them.

When she spoke of the program, it was written all over her face and in the sound of her enthusiasm that it was close to her heart.

There were three fairly newborn calves in the pen and three heifers. The babies each wore a calf skin over their backs like a second skin. He knew how it worked. She used the skin from a dead calf to cover an orphan so that the dead calf's mama would accept the orphan.. Sure, he knew how it worked, but when he watched Maddie talk about it, it hit him hard.

"This really means a lot to you, doesn't it?" he asked. Maddie felt things deep. It was obvious.

She was standing beside him and looking at the babies and mamas. "I can't stand for anything to be without a mom, so I love matching up orphans with new mamas." She waved a hand toward the cattle in the surrounding pasture. "All of those are new families." She smiled. "Isn't it cool?"

He was mesmerized by the intensity of her devotion. "You're a good mama, you know."

Shock flashed over her expression.

"Hey, don't look so shocked. You are. These are your babies, and you've matched them up and given them love and nurturing. You've taken a mama calf who longed for her baby and a baby who longed and needed a new mom to survive, and you've put them together. But they're still your babies."

"Hey, I'm a cattle woman, I'm not supposed to get so attached."

He nudged her arm and smiled. "But you do."

She nodded. "I do."

He couldn't help himself as he lifted his hand and

traced the profile of her face. "You have a big heart, Maddie."

She swallowed hard, drawing his gaze to her lips. His hand curled through her hair to gently cup the nape of her neck, and he tugged lightly. She stepped close, her gaze locked with his. His pulse thundered, and the need to kiss her was overwhelming.

This time they were alone in the middle of nowhere without an audience watching them. Other than Maddie's little bovine families.

He brushed his lips across hers, a driving need arose to taste the sweetness of her. An urgency he'd never felt before drove him as he realized he could kiss her forever. Almost instantly, a deep sigh whispered from her. She settled in his arms, her lips moving achingly soft against his, warm and answering as she took his breath away.

Cliff forgot everything but the feel of Maddie in his arms.

CHAPTER ELEVEN

Maddie hadn't forgotten the kiss in the truck. But it didn't compare to the tenderness of this kiss from the moment he pressed his lips to hers.

"Maddie," he whispered, trailing kisses along her jaw then back to her mouth as if he couldn't stay away too long. She knew she should pull away, run, flee before her heart did something irrevocable. But she couldn't. Just a little longer...

When he pulled away she was breathless. Dazed. And she had to stand very still while the world stopped spinning.

He raked a hand through his hair, his hat lay on the ground where she must have knocked it off.

"Maddie," he said, looking as stunned as she was.

She had to find footing. "I have to feed the babies." She strode to the rear of her truck. He followed her, and she could feel him watching her. Her hands trembled as she opened the cooler, and though she tried to make them stop, they kept on trembling as she pulled the two large bottles from the ice.

"You can be daddy for a day," she said, pushing one into his chest and letting go too quickly as she started for the pen. Luckily he grabbed it before it fell.

She led the way back to the barn and out to the other side where two baby calves waited in a small pen. They started bawling the moment they spotted her.

"Hey, little girls," she cooed, trying to focus on something besides than the feel of Cliff's kiss. She had to think. Had to calm down the chaos going on inside of her.

She reached into the pen to pet them, rubbing their ears as they tried to butt each other out of the way.

"Maddie, that kiss was incredible."

She didn't look at him. She couldn't. If she looked at him, he would see exactly how incredible she'd thought it was, too. If she looked at him, he would be able to see every hidden longing of her soul. If she looked at him, he would see the fear that gripped her. Could she risk that he wouldn't abandon her in the end too?

* * *

Think, Cliff.

Cliff knew that was easier said than done after having experienced the kiss of a lifetime. From the moment Maddie had rolled over in that dirt that first day and looked up at him with those fathomless green eyes, the fog he'd been moving in for days had started clearing out of his head. Every day he'd spent around her had brought him further out of any unresolved anger he'd felt toward his dad.

Now he was thinking only about what he wanted out of life.

And he knew he wanted Maddie in his life. His agent had called telling him they needed him in Mesquite the following weekend, and he'd told him to do what he had to, but that he wasn't coming back. Not full time and only when he wanted. He knew he'd lose his sponsors, but it had been a long haul, and he finally knew it was time. He trusted his agent to handle it with care and professionalism. He knew what was important in his life now and he was looking at her.

"Maddie, say something please."

She smiled over her shoulder, that vulnerable look still there behind her smile. "Poor things. They're twins. When their mother died, there wasn't a mama available, and all the other newborns were alive and well—which is a good thing. Anyway, if you'll help, we'll get these two rascals fed."

"Fine." He stepped up beside her, his arm brushing hers as he petted the one on her left and stuck the bottle through the gate. She was getting her emotions in check. The thought was like cheer in his heart.

He smiled as the twins latched onto the bottles and tried to yank them through the fence as they attacked the formula. He laughed, suddenly feeling like everything in the world was right.

"It's been a long time since I did this. I forgot how greedy they can be."

"It's an adventure."

"I have to agree."

She blushed.

The twins kicked each other again, and he chuckled along with Maddie before looking away. It took everything he had not to say anything else about the kiss. They'd talk about it when she was ready. Maybe he was moving too fast. It wasn't as if he'd chosen the pace though.

She looked past the pen to the land beyond, a contented expression on her face. "I've always wanted my own land, my own place. Always."

"Well, I'd say you've accomplished that."

The breeze lifted the edges of her blonde hair. "If C.C. hadn't made me a partner, I'd never have been able to afford anything near this size. But I'd have been content with something smaller. As long as I could feel like I owned a piece of Texas."

"We agree on that." He nudged her gently with his elbow, drawing her gaze to his again. "Texas is the place I knew I wanted to come back to. Rafe settling here helped me decide to try Mule Hollow."

The twins finished their bottles in that moment and immediately started head butting each other trying to reach the other's bottle.

She took the bottles and headed toward the truck.

"Do you know why your parents gave you up and let

you go into the foster system?" he asked, following her. Wanting more than ever to know more about her.

"No."

The sharp, dead way she said no red-flagged it as a subject that still hurt.

She moistened her lips. Her expression tightened.

"The truth, I was a very sick baby abandoned on the doorstep of the post office when I was just a few weeks old. Like my mom went to mail a letter and walked off and forgot me."

Cliff's throat squeezed tight, and he hung his head, staring at his boots, hurting for Maddie. "Awe, Maddie. I'm so sorry."

A too-vivid picture of Maddie as an infant crying for her mama filled his mind and caused the backsides of his eyes to burn.

"What, what happened? Who found you?" he said, gravel in this throat.

"One of the mailmen. I was taken in by the state. As I said, I was a very sickly child. My immune system was compromised and almost non-existent. Because of that, I was weak and pale and in and out of the hospital. Anyway, that's my story. I was raised in an orphanage the first part of my life and later different foster homes."

Cliff felt as if someone had kicked him in the gut. "Are you all right now? You work like a pack mule."

"See. That is exactly why I don't talk about myself. I don't like everyone looking at me and feeling sorry for me. I'm fine. I'm strong, and I rarely get sick." She put distance between them. "I shouldn't have told you that." She headed to the truck cab. "Let's go back."

He stalked after her. "Maddie, no kid should have to go through what you went through. Yeah, it upsets me for you."

"Don't look at me that way. I can't deal with it."

She climbed into her truck and slammed the door. Cliff was left standing on the outside looking in.

If he lived to be a hundred, he'd never understand Maddie Rose.

He yanked open the door. "Get out of that truck."

"Don't you tell me what to do." She grabbed the steering wheel with both hands and stared straight ahead.

"Okay, that does it. I warned you." He reached into the truck and scooped her into his arms. She held on to the steering wheel until her hands slipped off. She was no match for him.

"Let go of me," she snapped, kicking as he pulled her out and then slammed the door with his boot.

Not sure what he was doing but not caring. All he wanted to do was hold her.

"Let me down, Cliff Masterson, or I'll kick you. I will."

He set her on her feet and dragged her against him, needing to feel her heartbeat against his. "Maddie, it's okay to let people get close." He rested his head on the top of hers and held her. She had gone still in his arms. Her heart was thundering; he could feel every angry beat of it.

"It makes me angry. And, yeah, I'd be telling a bald-faced lie if I said I didn't feel bad for you for what you went through. I do." She pushed against his chest on that. "But I'm more impressed with what you've become. Maddie, you are amazing."

He wished he had the right words to say.

The pressure eased, and he leaned his head back so he could see her. "Your past isn't you today." He'd come to terms with that for himself finally.

Looking into Maddie's beautiful face, all he wanted to do now was help her realize that.

* * *

Maddie fought the raw ache of tears that threatened to spill over the edges of her eyes and roll down her cheeks.

She wouldn't cry. This, too, was why she kept her mouth shut about her past. It wasn't good to drag her memories back there.

This was ridiculous. Why did talking about the past still affect her so? *Maybe because you don't talk about it. Ever.*

"Talk to me, Maddie. I'm your friend. Right?"

"I'm not sure calling us friends is the right term," she said, a husky laugh surprising her.

"Hey, I totally disagree with that. If you remember, I pulled you out from under Buford's hooves. And we did just share the kiss of a lifetime." The reminder of that kiss filled her thoughts, wiping everything else away.

She laughed, and his eyes twinkled.

"See there," he said gently. "I told you, we're friends.

A friend does whatever it takes to make a friend feel better."

"Cliff, I don't know. This is all happening so fast."

He kissed her forehead. "You feel it as much as I do. You can deny it and back away from it, but just so you know, I'm not one to back away from something like that. I'm a bull rider. I like danger." He grinned, looking cocky and heart-stoppingly handsome.

Maddie knew she could fall in love with Cliff. And he had a way of making her so angry but so...reckless. This was too much.

She'd been hurt so much growing up. So very much. She backed up to the truck, and he placed his hands on either side of her shoulders. He was going to kiss her again.

"Cliff, I don't really know what to do about you. I have trouble opening up. Trusting."

He smiled and dipped his head and stole a swift gentle kiss. "Be my friend. Let me be there for you."

She nodded. Feeling overwhelmed.

He smiled. "And let me take you to the theater tomorrow night like we planned."

She couldn't say anything, just looked at him.

"And Maddie, don't be afraid of me. I wouldn't hurt you for the world."

He dipped in for another kiss, and it didn't even occur to her to push him away. Instead she cupped his jaw with her hands and returned the kiss.

When he had kissed her breathless and pulled back, she smiled shakily at him. "Okay, the theater is still on."

CHAPTER TWELVE

Maddie rolled over in bed and stuffed her face in the pillow. She'd agreed to a date with Cliff—after he'd curled her toes with a kiss that lingered on her lips even now.

She would never, never, *never* forget that kiss.

The feel of his arms, the taste of mint, the feel of a smile as it rippled through her hours afterward they'd parted.

She was petrified.

She was used to making herself be strong. To hide the fear.

Cliff didn't let her hide inside herself. He'd pushed her to open up because he cared. And then he'd refused to let her close him out after she'd told him her past.

For all the hard-working cowgirl she was, no one would guess how vulnerable she was on the inside. While she craved her own family, she couldn't help but feel she wasn't worthy of one.

Yet just thinking about the gentle way he'd kissed her had her insides melting all over again. Looking into his eyes, she'd believed him when he'd said he wouldn't hurt her. He'd been trying to keep her from hurting herself since the moment they'd met, so it was easy to believe him.

Only problem, he had no idea how tender her heart was. For a girl who'd never known what love was, not from anyone, stepping out to risk her heart was hard. She'd prayed for God to send her someone ever since she was a fourteen-year-old romantic up in the attic of one of the foster homes she happened to live at that summer. Could God have finally answered her prayers?

And so, as scared and uncertain as she felt, Maddie found herself smiling most of the week.

Was she ready for this? She honestly didn't know, but she couldn't resist.

* * *

Cliff had decided to buy the second property that he and Maddie had looked at. It was perfect, and he sensed Maddie liked it, too. It would be a few weeks until the closing, but Hailey had worked it out so that he could rent it until the contract went through. He spent the week cleaning it up.

Maddie came and helped him some, but even though she'd given him a look into her past, Maddie was still Maddie. She was still driven to push herself with her work, and he knew when to back off. She had obligations, and she was her own person.

He respected that about her.

Working at his new place gave him time away from her, too. Gave him time to think. It also minimized the possibility that he'd do or say something that would cause her to shut him out again.

They'd made progress, and he wasn't backtracking.

He was done with looking back and he planned to help Maddie do the same.

* * *

The big barn where the theater was set up sat a little ways off the road. On evenings when they held the play, cars and trucks would come from the surrounding counties in droves. It had become a small piece of Branson right there outside of Mule Hollow.

"Hey, there," Applegate Thornton boomed as they walked up. Maddie loved ol' App and his buddy Stanley, both so hard of hearing, their conversations tended to carry to everyone. They played more checkers at Sam's than ranched now that they were retired, and spent their weekend evenings handing out flyers for the shows and running the spotlights because they enjoyed it.

Stanley came hustling over, his plump face a full-blown grin. "Hey, Cliff, missed you at the checker game this mornin'." He sounded as if he were speaking through a megaphone.

Cliff mentioned that he'd played checkers a couple of mornings with App and Stanley, and they'd both beat him.

The perpetual frown that normally dominated Applegate's expression lifted as he looked from Cliff to Maddie. "'Bout time this here date night has finally arrived," he boomed for the world to hear.

People turned to look, and Maddie froze.

"It's a good night," Cliff said.

App shook his hand. "I figure you're one smart cookie to have this little gal on your arm."

"Yup." Stanley gave her a one-armed hug. "We were 'bout to decide she was gonna grow old and single because none of these cowpokes round here had sense enough to ask her out."

People were looking. Listening. Maddie tried to smile as she grabbed Cliff by the arm. "Thanks, fellas. We'll seat ourselves." Not waiting for more to be said, she dragged Cliff toward the first seats available. Plunking herself down, she yanked Cliff into the seat beside her.

He was chuckling and immediately draped his arm over the back of her chair, cupping her shoulder.

"Relax, Maddie, it's all right," he said, close to her ear.

She turned her head, bumping her nose into his unexpectedly. His eyes sparkled. "And, yes, they are all looking, but that's just fine with me."

Looking into his amazing, mischief-filled eyes, Maddie felt like the girl who was late to the party but won the door prize. Her insides trembled when he planted a kiss on the top of her nose and tugged her close as the lights began to dim.

In a daze, Maddie caught Esther Mae four rows up giving her a thumbs-up signal.

"Your friends are eating this up," he whispered, giving her shoulder a gentle squeeze as the cowboy band began playing the introduction music. "I'm glad you came with me."

In the darkness she inhaled his scent, rich spice and sun-warmed leather. "I'm glad to be here."

He touched his forehead to hers, gently caressed her shoulder and turned to enjoy the show.

A door in Maddie's heart cracked open, and she knew in that moment she could have sat that way for the rest of her life.

...And the voice of worry whispering she was getting in too deep—she ignored.

* * *

The next morning, they had the horses and travel supplies they were taking to the festival loaded before breakfast.

It didn't take thirty minutes to transform their patch of the festival into a riding school. And Cliff was amazed how many people were milling around by nine o'clock.

He enjoyed the way Maddie greeted the kids who came by and the way she obviously enjoyed their excitement about getting on a horse. Now that he had more insight into her background, he appreciated even more the connection she had toward these kids. Many of them probably hadn't ever been on a horse. It was only something they dreamed about, like she had. Thinking about that made him smile. Just as watching her now made him smile. Made him feel like a whole big world was opening up, and all they had to do was step into it together.

His phone buzzed, and he pulled it from his pocket. His smile faded when he saw his agent's name. As he hit the accept button, a sense of unease settled over him.

* * *

"Don't tug on the reins too hard. It hurts his mouth," Maddie told a little boy with stars in his eyes at the very idea of being on the back of a horse.

Seeing the kids on the horses reminded her of how she'd longed to ride one growing up. The kids energized her, as did the hum of awareness she felt when she was near Cliff.

Crazy partners! She'd wanted to both hug the guys last night and throttle them when she'd found them waiting up after the date. She was a grown woman, and she could take care of herself. And yet it had been touching to see them sitting there on the patio when Cliff took her home.

She had been quite certain that Cliff saw through their ruse of playing cards.

She glanced his way now. Standing behind the pens, he was talking on his cell phone, deep in conversation. Mule Hollow had terrible phone service, but there was a new tower, and reception was better than it used to be.

The intense, long conversation he was engaged in would not have been happening too long ago.

What were they talking about?

Pulling her attention from Cliff's pacing back and forth, she led the little boy, Randy, around the round pen, delighting in the pure joy in his laughter. The laughter faded in to the background as she glanced at Cliff again and saw him pocket his phone and hang his head.

What had happened?

Something was wrong.

She knew it before he motioned for her to come over. Her stomach quivered as she handed the lead rope to Chase.

"What's wrong," she asked after she climbed through the rungs on the portable round pen and met him.

"Maddie, I hate this, but I have to leave town for a few days. There's a PBR event that I can't get out of. I thought it would be no big deal to miss, but I was wrong. My sponsor is up in arms about it, and contractually, I'm bound."

"Wh-when do you leave?" she asked, forcing the words when they threatened to stick in the back of her throat.

"I have to grab my gear and head out now."

Her spirits deflated. "You have a career," she said, struggling not to overreact. But the voice of worry reared its ugly head. Had this settling down idea been only a whim?

Was he really not done with the road? Did his sponsors have so much control over him that he couldn't stop?

He touched her cheek, and the thrill of his touch skittered through her. Stiffening, she fought to harden her emotions to it.

"Go. I'll see you when I see you." Not that she had any hold on him. They'd been on one date. They'd only know each other two weeks.

Two weeks.

Two unbelievable, memorable, life-changing weeks.

He wrapped her in his arms and brushed a quick kiss across her lips. "I'll be back as soon as I can. You stay safe and out from under bulls' feet."

"Sure, just for you." She laughed huskily to hide the emotion threatening to burst from her.

It wasn't until he'd disappeared among the trucks heading for his own that she realized she hadn't told him to do the same.

Riding bulls for a living, no matter how good you were, was a dangerous job. A job that he loved.

Cliff Masterson was a bull rider. One of the best. And it was money made from surviving on the backs of those animals that was paying for the ranch he was buying. Could he really, truly turn his back on the career he loved and be satisfied to settle down away from the excitement of the ride?

Turning back to the round pen, she forced her nerves to settle and her mind away from Cliff.

She wasn't sure what she'd been thinking, but one thing was certain: she hadn't been using her head the last few days.

CHAPTER THIRTEEN

On Monday night, Cliff called. She hadn't heard from him either of the two nights after he left so quickly. When he finally did call she was miffed, not to mention hurt.

Maddie didn't mind the miffed part as much as she minded the hurt part. She did not like being hurt.

And that was what happened when you opened up your heart. You were vulnerable to hurt.

She hated being vulnerable. It brought back the helpless days of her childhood when she'd hoped and prayed that some family would come along and think she was worthy to be loved. When she'd see the hopeful couples come through the orphanage, she'd remember the thrill of anticipation that this might be the couple.

That this might be her family. And then she'd feel the devastating hurt when they passed her by for the child they'd chosen.

Maddie had cried herself to sleep so many times,

until finally she'd hardened her heart.

As an adult she'd shoved that pain to the furthest recesses of her heart and slammed an iron grill around it.

She hadn't let anything penetrate that grill until Cliff had blasted into her life, rescued her from Buford, then proceeded to knock down the barriers to her heart one by one—and stolen her heart.

What if he decided this had all been too fast?

That bulls were his life?

When he'd called, she hadn't talked to him long. The loudspeakers had been in the background, and he'd tried to explain over the noise that they were filming a show for one of the networks and that he'd been obligated to stay.

She tried to brush it off. After all, she'd only known Cliff a short time, too short of a time to put any real merit in a relationship building between them.

And yet, she knew somehow during all the sweet talk and those gentle ways, he'd slipped past her barriers and captured her heart. Her hope. Made her start dreaming of a life with him.

That alone irritated the fire out of her.

But it was undeniable.

How had she been so stupid? He'd never settled down before. Had she really believed that this time was different?

"I've got problems, girls," she confessed to the twins as they greedily attacked their bottles.

Memories of Cliff standing beside her as they fed

them weren't helping.

Needing to talk, she was glad she had the twins. "You gals are going to have to toughen up those hearts of yours. And don't let any young, good-looking bull come along and talk you into turning soft. No, ma'am, you stay strong or you'll get your heart broken."

Maddie knew it was easier to say than do. Because even though it had only been two weeks, two irritating, fun, exciting weeks, she knew the moment he'd kissed her that she had stepped into unchartered waters. There was nothing she could do but suffer now.

Suffer the uncertainty of whether he was coming back to Mule Hollow to stay, as he'd led her to believe. Or was he jumping back into bull riding with barely enough time to call her?

Maddie was afraid she'd been a fool. She'd known that no one in her life had ever believed she was worth sticking around for. Why had she let herself hope that Cliff was different?

A fool. That was exactly what she was.

* * *

"Hey, Cliff, you're up."

"Yeah, be right there," Cliff called over his shoulder, but let the phone keep ringing. After their call yesterday, he'd been increasingly worried about Maddie. "Come on, Maddie, pick up."

He'd been calling all day and no answer. The

answering machine clicked in, and he left a message again. "Maddie, I'm worried. Give me a call and let me know that you're okay."

He ended the call and then stared at the screen, as if doing that would will her to call him back instantly. She'd sounded closed off and distant the last time he'd spoken with her, like she'd been when he'd first met her. Like she was shutting him out.

Unease gripped him. He needed to talk to her.

"Cliff. You gonna ride?"

"Yeah, I'm riding." Stuffing the phone in his gear bag, he forced Maddie out of his mind and strode toward the bull with his number.

He'd called Rafe earlier to find out if he'd seen Maddie, and his brother had said she'd been acting kind of weird since he'd left.

Cliff hadn't liked that at all. He hadn't planned on being here for this three-day event. He'd tried to get out of it, but there were certain things that, unless you were injured and unable to ride, you couldn't get out of. He jogged up the metal steps and strode toward the chute. He hardly hesitated as he climbed over and planted his boots on the rails, straddling the bull but not yet lowering himself down to its back.

Cinnabar required full concentration if one was going to even attempt a six-second go, much less a full eight seconds without getting stomped.

"You okay, Cliff?" Brody asked. Brody Buchanan was a long-time friend from the circuit.

Cliff yanked at his gloves, making sure they were secure and gave a sharp nod.

"You don't look so good." Brody's piercing eyes searched his. "Come on, man, you've got to have your head on straight for this freight train, and you know it."

Cliff grunted, then gave Brody no choice but to let him go. He waited for Cinnabar to settle down, then lowered himself on top of the rusty red bull.

Cliff had to see Maddie. The best way to do that was to get this ride done so he could catch a flight home.

All he had to do was make this ride.

* * *

"Come on, girls, give a girl a break," Maddie said, playing tug-of-war with the twins on Monday evening. They were competing to see which one could yank off an arm first, or at least yank the bottle from her hand first.

"You are baby cows, not hogs," she said, feeling grumpy. She'd been unable to pull herself out of the low place she'd nosedived into since Cliff left town. Did the twins care that she felt lousy? Nope. They kept right on slobbering and yanking on the bottles like she'd done something to make them mad.

The overzealous calf gave a particularly hard tug, and Maddie lost her hold on the bottle. The calf raced across the pen, the big bottle dangling from her teeth. Why, the baby was so excited, she did a little kick with her hind legs. Distracted watching the calf, Maddie fumbled the other bottle when the other one gave it a yank and watched in dismay as the little glutton pranced off with her prize too.

Heaving out a big sigh, Maddie climbed through the rails and chased after the duo. She would have to wrestle the bottles away from them and then finish the feeding, because it was certain that they weren't going to get fed as the bottle dragged along in the dirt.

Heading toward the nearest one, she latched hold of the bottle, but the calf was not giving up on her prize easily. She dug in her hooves, gritted her pearly whites and held on. One minute Maddie was standing, and the next she was being yanked around. Her foot slipped in the soft ground, and she found herself face first in the dirt. It was a good thing her ribs were feeling better, she thought as she pushed herself to a sitting position.

"I leave for four days, and you're back swimming in the dirt."

At the husky drawl, Maddie's heart slowed and then picked up speed. She spun around to see Cliff grinning at her from the other side of the pen.

He looked so good, she almost forgot how mad she was. His jaw was covered in a five o'clock shadow that seemed to accentuate his dazzling smile and his twinkling eyes.

Goodness, she had to fight the urge to run over and throw her arms around him. She'd missed him more than she wanted to admit. More than she could believe.

She'd been wary of letting a man wiggle past her

defenses, and here he'd gone and done it. And done it good.

And now, she was terrified she couldn't live without him.

She was sitting in the dirt wanting to cry because she knew that falling in love with the twinkle-eyed cowboy grinning at her from across the arena fence had the ability to crush her world. And he'd done it in only two weeks' time!

What damage could he do if given longer?

Cliff climbed over the fence and strode toward her. Her heart fluttered like a panicked parakeet.

She finally scrambled up as the panic set in.

He stalked across the pen, his eyes turning serious as he came. "Maddie, why didn't you take my last calls? What's wrong? All I could think about was getting back here to see what was going on."

He was mere inches from her, and she planted a hand in the middle of his chest to keep him from wrapping those strong arms of his around her. "Stop," she commanded, having already learned that she didn't think well when he did that. "This moved too fast, Cliff."

"Love moves at its own pace, darlin', and that is just the way it is."

She narrowed her eyes, as if narrowing them would narrow the gap trying to pull open in her heart. Her stinkin' heart lurched despite the battle she was putting up. "Don't sweet talk me. You move too fast. How am I supposed to believe you haven't dipped into Mule Hollow like a whirlwind before spinning off to new places? Because I know your personality is too strong to settle for the quiet life we all live here."

His grin slashed cocky and crooked. "See there, already you know me like it's been forever. Believe me, darlin', there's going to be excitement in our lives. Don't you doubt it. And I'm not talkin' about the wild bulls we're going to raise. God didn't say when a man and woman got married that life lost its luster."

Her insides rolled over like a puppy begging for a belly rub at the look in his eyes. She knew life being married to Cliff wouldn't be dull or lackluster. It would be passionate and fun, and there would be plenty of head butting too. If the matchmakers liked sparks, well, Maddie had no doubt that she and Cliff could start a forest fire with the ones they'd raise. It was him she worried about. Would she be woman enough to hold him if she was strong enough to allow her heart to let him in?

"We need to slow down," she snapped, self-preservation kicking in when she felt the chink in her armor crack a little wider.

Cliff stepped up and took her in his arms. She knew if he kissed her, she'd melt like butter again.

He kissed the tip of her nose. Her breath caught in her throat, and her knees felt weak.

"I love you, Maddie Rose. I've told you before I'm a man who knows what he wants, and I'm planning on spending the rest of my life proving to you that I'm a man of my word."

Maddie's world started spinning. "I'm afraid, Cliff. There, I've admitted it."

He lifted her chin to gaze into her eyes. "Then we'll slow down, take it slow. It'll be hard for me, but I'll do it because you need time. I understand that." He kissed her forehead.

She could feel his heartbeat so strong against her hand. She wanted to believe him so badly, it hurt. She'd longed her whole life to be loved.

"Maddie, you changed my world from the moment I saw you. And the moment I first kissed you, I knew you were the woman for me. You knew it, too. We'll take all the time you need. Just know I'm the man who is going to give you the family you've always wanted. I've been waiting my whole life to find you. And I'll wait my whole life to have you, if that's what it takes."

He had looked into her soul and read exactly what she'd been thinking. Knew exactly what her hopes and dreams were. Did it really matter if he'd known her a week or fifty-two?

"You would do that? But your sponsors? Your contracts?"

His gaze gentled and shined with love. "This event fulfilled my contract. They offered me another one, but I told them thanks, but no thanks. I've got new dreams now, Maddie. And I'll do whatever it takes for you to know that I'm the man who loves you and who'll love you always with every breath I breathe. Whatever it takes to prove, that I'll do."

Maddie stared into his beautiful eyes and believed him. He'd actually chosen to come back to her. She loved this man. Suddenly, spontaneously, she shocked herself by springing to her tiptoes and planting her lips on his.

If she'd wanted to hold off and be cautious, this was not the way to do it. But Maddie had been cautious all her life, and it hit her as he'd said he'd wait that for the first time in her life she didn't want to wait. Her lips melted to Cliff's and molded to his like they'd been made for each other. And she was convinced they had been. God was one smart cookie.

Her arms wound themselves around Cliff's neck, and she tugged him closer. He didn't hesitate to join in, kissing her with power and tenderness and promise of things to come.

"Maddie," he growled, pulling back finally, his heart thundering against her own. "What are you telling me with this kiss? Because I'm telling you, that this is powerful, and I don't want to misunderstand."

"I'm *saying* that I've been waiting for love my entire life. Is this irresponsible? Some might say so, but I know that many happily-ever-after, true-life love stories have been love at first sight—"

"Or first fight," he chuckled.

"That is for certain." She grinned, her heart swelling with hope and love and dreams...new dreams of a ranch they'd build together and a family they'd raise.

Cupping her face between his hands, he stared with loving intensity into hers. "Darlin', will you marry me?

Now or later, I simply want to know you're going to be mine."

She loved the sound of that. "Yes, I love you, Cliff with all my heart."

"Yes!" The smile that spread over his face filled every dark corner of her soul. "Maddie, I promise to guard your precious heart with my love for the rest of my life."

With that, he lowered his lips to hers and, Maddie knew she was home at last...

Chapter Excerpt from

RAFE

New Horizon Ranch, Book Two

CHAPTER ONE

A human-size, fluffy, pink-tailed bunny on the side of the road was the last thing Rafe Masterson expected to see on his way to his brother's engagement party.

He squinted through the sun's rays. "Surely not—" he said, driving closer. But, yup, that was definitely the furry white rump of a bunny bent over the backend of the trunk of the broke down sports car. The critter had a flat tire.

Rafe pressed the brake as the cotton tail wiggled and the bunny popped to a standing position, no bunny head attached. Instead, sun-kissed red hair splayed down the furry back almost touching the cotton tail. Rafe stomped harder on the brake just as Bunny Woman propped one oversized rabbit's foot on the bumper of the car and yanked hard on the spare tire. Instantly it popped free, sending Bunny Woman and the tire she was clutching stumbling backwards like a drunk on Saturday night.

She tripped over her feet and fell forward on top of the tire, her bunny tail flopping in the breeze just as Rafe barreled from his truck and raced to help. All the while thinking his brother Cliff and his ranch partners weren't going to believe his reason for being late to Cliff's engagement dinner party.

He skidded to a halt just as the redhead rolled off the tire onto her back, bunny feet pointing to the sky by a good eighteen inches. They were huge.

"Are you okay?" He gaped at the massive feet and then the gigantic white belly that sloped to the prettiest, *maddest* bunny he'd ever seen.

"Oh sure," she grunted, magnificent green eyes flashing brilliant as a neon sign. "I'm just peachy wonderful." She struggled to sit up, all the while scowling.

Rafe dropped to one knee and grabbed hold of her fuzzy arm to assist her in her effort. "I hate to break it to you, but you don't look too peachy wonderful to me. You look hotter than a firecracker and a good bit uncomfortable." He held back a chuckle. "I'll fix your tire--"

"Thanks, but no thanks," she snapped. "Contrary to what it looks like, I can fix my own tire. I thank you for stopping, but I don't need a man to fix my flat." Under her breath, she added, "or anything else."

"Shew, you are miffed about something." He tugged her to her feet without asking if she wanted him to.

"Thanks," she said, then stalked away.

He watched while she clomped toward her car, her feet, thick and long, made splatting sounds on the pavement.

"Hey, hold up," he called, striding to catch her.

She didn't answer. Instead she started digging around inside the trunk, that pink bunny tail flopping sassily with every movement.

Whew, she was mad at someone, and he'd put money on that someone being a man. "I really don't mind helping." He gave her his best grin and placed one hand on rim of the trunk. "It would be a pity for you to get your fur all messed up," he drawled and shot her a smile. "And I hate to mention it, but those feet are probably going to get in your way."

A funny expression on her face, and she looked down at her feet, almost as if she'd forgotten about them. Which was understandable since her belly was so big she couldn't actually *see* her feet. How had she driven the car this far?

She bent forward to see more than her toes. "They roll up—"

"Hand it over, Flossy." Rafe reached for the tire tool. "In Texas when we see a lady or a bunny in distress we stop and help."

Her eyes flashed as his hand wrapped around it. She tugged and held on. He gave her a stern look.

"I'm not gonna stand here and watch you pass out changing that tire--or attempting to change it. From the looks of your cheeks, you won't last long."

"I don't need you," she said.

"Yes, you do." Rafe was known for getting a job done, and he was in serious danger of getting lost in her green eyes and forgetting about everything. "If it helps calm your nerves or anything, I'll introduce myself. I'm Rafe Masterson. I'm part owner of New Horizon Ranch, and I'm well known in Mule Hollow and the surrounding county. You can trust me."

"O-kay." She sighed, looking weary with her pink cheeks and damp skin. "I concede to the cowboy." She let go of the jack. "And thank you."

He grinned. He couldn't help it as he tipped his hat. "A very smart move. And may I ask your name?"

"Sadie. Sadie Archer"

"Nice to meet you, Sadie."

He turned and set to work, not wanting her to grab hold of the jack again. His mind was racing with questions about Sadie the bunny, but he focused on getting the car jacked up. She moved over to the tire and rolled it in his direction. The fact that she was a large white bunny was still making him want to chuckle, but his curiosity had blown all out of proportion about why in the world she was in the funny getup.

"Are you sure you have time to do this?" she asked, rolling the tire to a stop. "You look like you're all dressed up for a date or something?"

Wondering about her, he'd completely forgotten about Maggie and Cliff's party. "I'm heading to my brother's engagement party. But it'll be fine. I'll call him and let him know I'm running a little late."

She bit her lip and pushed her crimson bangs off her moist forehead.

The sun sizzled here in the middle of Texas at four, even on a mid-September afternoon, and he didn't know how long she'd been out in it before he arrived.

"That suit has to be smothering you. Can't you take it off?"

"Um, no. I can't." She plucked at a piece of lifeless white belly fur. "Believe me, if I could, I would. But I'm fine."

"You don't look fine. You look like you're going to fall over any moment from overheating." He was already damp, and he was only wearing a starched western dress shirt and jeans, no fur. Her cheeks were rapidly turning hot pink.

"I said I was fine."

"Yeah, right." He could look at her and tell that wasn't so. Working fast, he had the flat tire off and the spare in place within a few minutes. The last thing he needed was for her to pass out on him from heat exhaustion. "Done." He let the jack down. "Now, jump inside the car and get some air going to cool those pretty cheeks off."

Looking less perky than she had when he first arrived, she didn't bother to protest. Instead, she trudged over and sank into her seat. That hairy suit had to be getting heavier by the minute. In a moment, he heard the AC blowing full blast. He should have had her sitting in there the whole time, or in his truck. But then as stubborn as she seemed, he figured she probably wouldn't have gotten out of the heat while a complete stranger did work for her.

He dusted off his hands. His job was done, and he had a party to get to, but he didn't feel comfortable leaving her yet. He rested an arm on the top of the door and stared down at her. "Do you need help?"

"You already helped enou--"

"No, I mean are you in trouble?" he asked, gently. "Something doesn't seem right about this situation." And he wasn't one to beat around the bush. He'd been through a lot in his life, and something about her reminded him of the way his mother used to look. Back when he was a kid and home life was hell. Literally. With a no account father she'd protected over and over again, he and his twin brother, Cliff, had been forced to endure a home life that still haunted him in many ways.

He did not take a woman in trouble lightly.

Sadie rubbed her hand on her furry thigh then hesitantly raised her eyes to his. "I'm fine. Do you know if anyone is hiring in Mule Hollow? I could use a job."

Rafe's stomach dipped, and his palms dampened as he look into those eyes. "Me. I mean our ranch is looking for help."

She studied him, sparks flashing in her eyes. "Seriously, or are you just saying that?"

"No, I'm not," he said too quickly, suddenly for some unexplainable reason wanting her to accept his help. "To be honest, we don't have any need for a five-foot-four-inch bunny, but we could sure use a…a *cook*. Can you cook?"

Her gaze turned probing. Or was that skeptical. "It's not my strong point, but I can manage."

Rafe figured she could have told him she burned toast and scorched eggs and he'd have been fine with that. The fact that she was being honest about her ability was a plus.

"Then you're hired."

Sadie couldn't believe what she was considering. Where had the needing a job bit come from in the first place? Probably because the bunny suit was frying her from the inside out, and the sun was baking her brain.

That and the fact that she still hadn't gotten over the fact that she'd found her fiancé kissing one of her best friends four hours ago.

She closed her eyes and tried to settle the turmoil crashing around inside of her. This had been the worst day of her life, and she'd just complicated it more by mentioning she needed a job. But that was the weird part. She *didn't* need a job, did she? She just needed time.

Time to figure out how she'd made such a mess of her life.

She was a strong, independent woman, so how could she have let her relationship with Andrew go this far in the first place?

Because you were tired of waiting while everyone around you got married and had babies.

She sighed, knowing the voice in her heart spoke the truth.

Her stomach churned as she looked up at Rafe Masterson. Why had she mentioned this to him, a total stranger? She should just drive on. "Does being the cook on a ranch come with room and board?" Being a cook on this cowboy's ranch would give her the time she needed to get her thoughts together and figure out what her next move should be.

No one would look for her on a ranch, would they?

She was a city girl, born and bred. And everyone who knew her understood this.

No, they'd look for her anywhere but on a cattle ranch.

"Sure it does." The amazingly handsome cowboy stared down at her, and his smoldering gaze dug into her like the tabs on a lie detector machine. Oddly enough, Sadie was tempted to spill her very bad and personal day to the man on the spot.

"Then I'll take the job." She held out her hand to shake on the deal, and he took hers in his larger one. His callused palm sent a jolt of awareness through her. But in its shocking wake, there was also a sense of reassuring strength in his touch. It resonated from his amazing eyes.

"Good," he said, continuing to hold her hand for a moment. "If you want to follow me to the ranch, I'll show you where you'll be working, and I'll introduce you to my other four partners and my brother."

"Sure, that sounds good." What was she doing? The man was chivalrous, good-looking and thoughtful. But still, was she really about to accept a job from a total stranger because her life was in the dumps?

New Horizon Ranch Series
Her Texas Cowboy (Book 1)
Rafe (Book 2)
Chase (Book 3)
Ty (Book 4)
Dalton (Book 5)
Treb (Book 6)
Maddie's Secret Baby (Book 7)
Austin (Book 8)

More Books by Debra Clopton

Sunset Bay Romance
Longing for Forever (Book 1)
Longing for a Hero (Book 2)
Longing for Love (Book 3)
Longing for Ever-After (Book 4)
Longing for You (Book 5)

Texas Brides & Bachelors
Heart of a Cowboy (Book 1)
Trust of a Cowboy (Book 2)
True Love of a Cowboy (Book 3)

New Horizon Ranch Series
Her Texas Cowboy (Book 1)
Rafe (Book 2)
Chase (Book 3)
Ty (Book 4)
Dalton (Book 5)
Treb (Book 6)
Maddie's Secret Baby (Book 7)
Austin (Book 8)

Cowboys of Ransom Creek
Her Cowboy Hero (Book 1)
The Cowboy's Bride for Hire (Book 2)
Cooper: Charmed by the Cowboy (Book 3)
Shane: The Cowboy's Junk-Store Princess (Book 4)
Vance: Her Second-Chance Cowboy (Book 5)
Drake: The Cowboy and Maisy Love (Book 6)
Brice: Not Quite Looking for a Family (Book 7)

Turner Creek Ranch Series
Treasure Me, Cowboy (Book 1)
Rescue Me, Cowboy (Book 2)
Complete Me, Cowboy (Book 3)
Sweet Talk Me, Cowboy (Book 4)

Texas Matchmaker Series
Dream With Me, Cowboy (Book 1)
Be My Love, Cowboy (Book 2)
This Heart's Yours, Cowboy (Book 3)
Hold Me, Cowboy (Book 4)
Be Mine, Cowboy (Book 5)
Marry Me, Cowboy (Book 6)
Cherish Me, Cowboy (Book 7)
Surprise Me, Cowboy (Book 8)
Serenade Me, Cowboy (Book 9)
Return To Me, Cowboy (Book 10)
Love Me, Cowboy (Book 11)
Ride With Me, Cowboy (Book 12)
Dance With Me, Cowboy (Book 13)

Windswept Bay Series
From This Moment On (Book 1)
Somewhere With You (Book 2)
With This Kiss (Book 3)
Forever and For Always (Book 4)
Holding Out For Love (Book 5)
With This Ring (Book 6)
With This Promise (Book 7)
With This Pledge (Book 8)
With This Wish (Book 9)
With This Forever (Book 10)
With This Vow (Book 11)

About the Author

Bestselling author Debra Clopton has sold over 2.5 million books. Her book OPERATION: MARRIED BY CHRISTMAS has been optioned for an ABC Family Movie. Debra is known for her contemporary, western romances, Texas cowboys and feisty heroines. Sweet romance and humor are always intertwined to make readers smile. A sixth generation Texan she lives with her husband on a ranch deep in the heart of Texas. She loves being contacted by readers.

Visit Debra's website at www.debraclopton.com

Sign up for Debra's newsletter at www.debraclopton.com/contest/

Check out her Facebook at www.facebook.com/debra.clopton.5

Follow her on Twitter at @debraclopton

Contact her at debraclopton@ymail.com

If you enjoyed reading *Cowboy Up Boxed Set* I would appreciate it if you would help others enjoy this book, too.

Recommend it. Please help other readers find this book by recommending it to friends, reader's groups and discussion boards.

Review it. Please tell other readers why you liked this book by reviewing it on the retail site you purchased it from or Goodreads. If you do write a review, please send an email to debraclopton@ymail.com so I can thank you with a personal email. Or visit me at: www.debraclopton.com.

www.ingramcontent.com/pod-product-compliance
Lightning Source LLC
Chambersburg PA
CBHW070319190726
48291CB00014B/2280